Praise for *You Will Surely Not Die: Adam and Eve Journey to Missouri* by Beth Woods

You Will Surely Not Die provides an interesting insight into eternity. Regardless of your religious beliefs, the thought that this life continues, that we will see those we have loved and lost, and that the beauty of this earth is just a small piece of what lies beyond is something we all wonder about. Jordan's journey with Duchenne muscular dystrophy brings some of these concerns to light in a thought-provoking way.

—**Pat Furlong,
President and CEO of Parent Project
Muscular Dystrophy**

What we do with our grief is what we will have done with our lives. In *You Will Surely Not Die*, Beth Woods brings her own grappling with love and loss to a deeply attentive character sketch of a lovely young man named Jordan and the blessing he's determined to be to those he loves.

—**David Dark,
author of *The Sacredness of
Questioning Everything***

You Will Surely Not Die

Adam and Eve Journey to Missouri

2

Beth Woods

You Will Surely Not Die 2: Adam and Eve Journey to Missouri
Copyright © 2019 by Beth Woods
Published by Deep River Books
Sisters, Oregon
www.deepriverbooks.com

All rights reserved. No part of this book may be reproduced or transmitted in any form or by any means, electronic or mechanical, including photocopying and recording, or by any information storage and retrieval system, without permission in writing from the publisher.

Unless otherwise indicated, all Scripture quotations are taken from the Holy Bible, New Living Translation, copyright © 1996, 2004, 2007, 2013 by Tyndale House Foundation. Used by permission of Tyndale House Publishers, Inc., Carol Stream, Illinois 60188. All rights reserved.

Scripture quotation marked NKJV are taken from The Holy Bible, New King James Version®.

Copyright © 1982 by Thomas Nelson, Inc. Used by permission. All rights reserved.

ISBN – 13: 9781632695185
Library of Congress: 2019913437

Printed in the USA

Cover design by Joe Bailen, Contajus Designs

Dedication

This novel is dedicated to Seph Ware,
an incredible kid with an amazing outlook on life.

Author's Note

Please allow me to take a minute to state the obvious. This is a work of fiction. I am not intending to rewrite the holy and inerrant words of Scripture. I am not trying to change anyone's perception of the accounts of creation and devastation portrayed in the first eight chapters of Genesis. I believe that the Bible is the inspired Word of God and that every page describes people and events that were completely under the dominion of the one true God of the universe, the God of Abraham, Isaac, and Jacob.

We are warned several times not to add to or subtract from the Scriptures. It is not within our ability to pick and choose sections that we like or choose to believe and obey, only to cast others aside without consequence. Deuteronomy 4:2, Deuteronomy 12:32, and Proverbs 30:5–6 tell us this with absolute clarity. My intention is to commit neither of these atrocities. I am merely attempting to entertain an audience with a story based on a ridiculous premise, sparked by the Bible but not intended to conflict with it, with the intention of creating memorable characters and situations.

Beth Woods

Acknowledgments

The character of Jordan is loosely based on a sixteen-year-old Duchenne muscular dystrophy patient, Seph (Joseph) Ware, whom I was fortunate enough to know as a student in my public school geometry classroom and as a member of my Scholastic Bowl team. In my imagination I created all scenarios described in this novel; they do not reflect any factual events, although the boys who attended the fictional retreat weekend were given names of real-life DMD patients who are special to Seph and his mother, Lori.

DMD is estimated to affect about one in five thousand males at birth. Although females are generally carriers with no observable symptoms, in rare instances they are diagnosed with DMD as well.

When Seph was diagnosed at the age of three, his parents were told that he would not see his eighteenth birthday. Since then however, medical advancements, especially in the area of home ventilation systems, have increased the life expectancy of these patients to an average of twenty-six years; some live into their thirties and beyond.

When I began this project, Seph's mother was grieving over the loss of Danny, a precious little round-faced boy six months younger than her son. I never met the dark-haired Rutgers fan from New Jersey, but from pictures of Danny on Facebook and stories that Lori and Seph told me, I realize that I missed an opportunity to know an incredible young man. I extend my most sincere best wishes to Danny's family, and I hope that I portrayed my fictional version of him in a way that brings a smile to your face and the memory of his.

Chapter 1

Eve was trying her hardest to walk through the waist-deep water with her fins still on, but as she emerged out of the Red Sea it became too difficult. She sighed, spun around, and plopped down on the sandy bottom to pull them off. Adam, who came up behind her, had already removed his fins in deeper water. He couldn't help but laugh at his wife.

"Having trouble, hon?"

Eve looked up at him and flicked some water in his direction.

Adam circled around behind his wife and grabbed her air tank by the knob on the top. "Unhook your BC, and I'll take this weight off for you. It'll make it a lot easier to climb out."

Eve pinched a couple of sets of clips on her BCD and pulled the Velcro waist strap loose so that she could wriggle free from the vest's armholes. Adam lifted the air tank. With the bulky equipment removed, she was able to get the fins off and stand with ease. She was grateful for the help but could have managed without it. "You know dear, in today's world men acknowledge that women can do things like that for themselves."

"You want to carry it? It weighs a ton."

"Oh goodness no, I don't want to carry it. Just appreciating my old fashion guy, that's all!" Eve knew there was nothing Adam wouldn't do for her, and, although she was a strong, capable woman, she appreciated the man who had taken care of her for almost six thousand years.

The two climbed up the steep, sandy slope to the beach and trudged to a vacant picnic table close to the road. Several members from their group had already started putting their SCUBA gear on the trailer parked nearby and had started to pull on dry clothes. Two guides were talking about the fact that they had never in their lives seen so many schools of fish on one dive, not to mention the turtles and rays. Eve smiled as if she knew the reason for that and shifted her attention to a young boy she had enjoyed watching all day.

"I like boat diving better, Dad. You know, like we did in the Adriatic last year."

"It is easier getting in and out of the water, I'll give you that," his dad replied, struggling with the equipment.

"I liked the boat ride. Remember, we saw flying fish and had cookies."

"Sure did. As I remember, the dive was good too. There are advantages to both types, I guess. Here I think most of the dive companies do shore diving because once you get away from the shore it gets too deep to explore. Taking a boat out really isn't needed."

The dark-haired Italian boy noticed Eve was listening to their conversation and said to her, "Did you see that spotted ray? It was huge!"

Eve smiled at the outgoing youngster and responded in flawless Italian, "I did. Did you see the giant moray?"

"Yeah! He looked mean."

"They can be if provoked, but that's just the face they have," Eve said gently. "I saw a dive master actually pet a green moray on a dive once. It followed us for the rest of the trip."

"No way! That would never happen," the boy responded.

"It did. I promise. I suspect that dive master had a prior relationship with it though. Maybe he had regularly fed the eel before, and it had learned to trust him. I don't know, but I really did see that one time in the Caribbean. That green moray loved that diver," Eve laughed. "I guess that's amoré!"

The boy laughed at the corny attempt to use Italian in a fish pun. "Whatever! I stayed clear of the one today. He was scary. I really wanted to see a dugong and a crocodile fish, but I didn't see either one."

"He read about them in school," his father offered.

"Maybe next time," she replied to the boy. "I bet you found Nemo, though, didn't you?"

"Sure did. I saw several clownfish." The boy laughed and turned back to his father, who started quizzing his son on the topography. Eve continued to listen to the exchange.

"Let's see what you can remember. What's over there?"

"All of that, down as far as you can see, is Saudi Arabia."

"Right. What is up there?"

"Jordan. We were there last night in Aqaba."

"And next to it, coming this way?"

"Israel, and this entire side, all the way down, is Egypt."

"You're doing great. Now the last question: What is this body of water called?"

"The Gulf of Aqaba. It is on the east side of the Sinai Peninsula and is an upper section of the Red Sea. Satisfied?"

"Yeah. I'll stop trying to teach you things for a while now."

"I bet you can't make it twenty minutes," the boy laughed.

Adam walked up with the top portion of his wet suit bunched around his waist, half a sandwich hanging out of his mouth, and their dry bag in his hand. He took a big bite and when he was able he said, "I found our bag in the back of the truck. What do you need?"

"Just help me out of this thing first," she replied.

Adam put the bag down, shoved the rest of the sandwich in his mouth and pulled the zipper cord down the back of her suit. He helped her to pull her arms out of the tight, sticky sleeves, and when the top half was bunched around her middle like his was, he reached into the bag and pulled out a towel for her.

"How did the mustache sealer work?" Eve asked her husband.

"Ok, I guess. I think if I were to go diving more often, I would have to shave the whole works off, but for today it was fine. It leaked some, but I got used to the little bit of slosh in the bottom of my mask. I could still see what I needed to."

"Good thing we're not diving more," Eve chuckled as she continued to dry off her bathing suit. "I like this look. The short-trimmed beard looks nice on you."

He just replied with a smile and watched her without comment as she dabbed her face with the towel and pulled the hairband from her long brown hair. She raked her fingers through it then tied it back up and was almost feeling put back together when the guide came over and offered them both a container of orange slices and pineapple chunks. The Egyptian's eyes lingered on Eve for several moments longer than what she felt was appropriate, but she smiled, took slices of each fruit, and nodded her head appreciatively. The guide was barely holding up his end of a conversation with one of the divers, but she didn't want to interrupt by offering verbal thanks anyway.

"But you know where it is, right?" the diver asked trailing along behind the guide.

"Generally, but not really, and anyway it is too far from here. And you'd need a boat to do it right, and it will take some time." The guide was obviously interested in leaving the conversation and hurried over to another diver to offer fruit.

Eve thought the man looked frustrated, but she sensed he was attempting to be content when he looked at her and smiled. He sat down beside her and looked out at the water. "Beautiful, isn't it?"

"I couldn't agree more. Your name is Michael, right?" Eve asked.

"That's right. Did you get any good pictures when we were down there?" he asked, eying the underwater dive camera that had been carefully placed beside her on the bench.

"I don't know. Let's see. Adam, have you had a chance to look at the shots you took?"

"Not yet. I think they want us in the van as soon as we get dried off. We can all look at it together when we get back to the shop."

The seven divers piled into a van, and the guides got into a small truck, its bed filled with empty air tanks, BCDs, fins, weights, masks, dry bags, and coolers. When they got back to the shop, the guide showed Adam how to hook his camera to the widescreen television on the wall, and the group gathered around to see some of the shots from their 53-minute underwater expedition. Divers laughed when they saw themselves and sounded collective "ooohs" and "aaaahs" when something interesting appeared. Several divers asked Adam if they could buy some of the pictures from him. Adam got email addresses and agreed to send copies to whoever wanted them, free of charge. Nobody was more excited than the Italian boy's father since Adam had happened to photograph his son upside-down and face-to-face with a turtle almost as big as he was.

As the two biblical icons left the dive shop, Eve expressed her confusion. "Do you have any idea at all?" she asked Adam. "I listened to every conversation around me all day and nothing stood out."

"With me either. I haven't a clue why God sent us on that trip. Maybe it will be revealed when I send these pictures out."

"Maybe," Eve agreed. "I'm not complaining though. It isn't often we go someplace exotic like this and enjoy ourselves without any apparent responsibility. It was a momentous day."

"Let's keep that going. I want to go to Eilat tonight. You up for that? I hear they have a boardwalk with lots of food and shops and that slingshot ride that Dale told us about."

"That sounds great! Sounds like a day of celebrations. I wonder if it's my birthday. Let's just say it is."

"Wanna talk about how old you will be turning if it is?"

"Not at all. Anyway, I've lost count," Eve laughed.

"Well let me just say that you look amazing for someone turning roughly six thousand years old."

Eve slapped him playfully. "You don't look so bad either, old man. And, I might add, you are even older than I am."

"Yeah, but by less than a day."

"Older is older, and I am never going to let you forget it."

Chapter 2

"I didn't say anything, Cole, I swear it."

"I know you did. Lucy would never snub me like that."

"Dude, she just had something else on her mind, that's all. She probably didn't even see you."

"Chris, she saw me. She looked mad. She just got home from college last night, so there is no way she would have heard about what I did at that party if you hadn't told her."

"I didn't say anything. I told you that. Maybe you should be more careful about who you're seen cozying up to if you are so afraid of what people are going to say. Maybe somebody posted a picture of you or something, but I didn't do it."

"So you're saying she knows?"

"Come on, man. Drop it. I didn't say anything. Lucy isn't mad at you. Just calm down."

"Whatever. I'm going home."

"See ya," Christopher said weakly to his best friend of ten years. As a last-ditch effort to smooth things over, he offered, "You know if you had any chance at all with my sister, I would talk to her for you."

The car door slammed, and Cole was gone. Christopher noticed the black clouds building in the distance, turned to go back in the house and sighed. Living in Tornado Alley was never boring in the springtime. No matter how menacing the sky looked, the threat of a long-term squabble with Cole bothered him more. All he could think about was that he hoped Lucy hadn't heard any of the exchange so that he wouldn't have to choose between explaining it to her or lying about it. He had just come in the door when his mom yelled from the kitchen.

"Christopher, is that you?"

"Yeah, Ma."

"I thought I heard Cole. Is he staying for dinner? It's almost ready."

"No, not tonight. I think Jen's coming over in about an hour though," Christopher yelled back as he headed to the kitchen to join her and see what unguarded treats there were to nibble on.

After dinner, Christopher's head was still hurting. He hated it when Cole was mad at him, and he knew plenty well from experience that things would not smooth over until he figured out a way to make it happen. Thankfully, he thought, Jen was coming over, and she always had such a nice way of taking his mind off of everything else. They had been together for almost two years, and Christopher could see their future together more clearly than he would admit. He had known since the first time he kissed her that they would be together forever, and, although they had never discussed wedding bells or babies, he knew that she knew it too.

He heard a knock on his bedroom door and opened his eyes, sat up on his bed, and took his headphones off. Jennifer opened the door and peeked in at Christopher who smiled in return.

"Hey," she said as she closed the door behind her. "It is getting crazy outside. The sky is black and the wind almost knocked me over when I was coming up the walk."

"Hi," he said warmly. "I know. Life in Tornado Alley is never dull. Not long ago I had to turn up the music to keep the whistling wind from being a problem." Not even a smile. He tried again for a reaction. "I heard there was an F-3 in Fayetteville earlier and headed this way. I've seen worse though." She hadn't even taken a step toward him. Were those tears in her eyes? "What's wrong, Jen?"

She came over slowly, bent at the waist to give him a quick peck, and sat down beside him on the bed. "I'm sure it will pass over. I think they said it would be downgraded within the hour. Chris, I need to talk to you about something." The rain pelted the window.

"What's wrong? What happened? Are you okay?"

"Nothing happened; I'm fine. Listen, I just have some decisions to make, and Mom and Dad have been all over me lately to figure things out." Jennifer paused for a long moment. "I got accepted at Mizzou."

"University of Missouri? That's great!" Christopher exclaimed, trying his hardest to sound excited for her. "Your first choice. When did you find out?"

"Yesterday, when I got home from school. I wanted to tell you then, but . . ." Her voice trailed off, and Christopher covered her hand with his.

"But you wanted to tell me in person that you have decided to go there?" Jennifer pulled her hand away and stood up. Chris couldn't help but feel she was just pretending to be interested in something on his desk that she needed to investigate. Why was she trying to get away from him?

She took a deep breath and turned to him with what he sensed was renewed conviction in her voice. "Yeah. I know we talked about going to C of O together, but you know that's a pipe dream. With the no-tuition policy, only 12 percent of applications are granted acceptance to the College of the Ozarks.

The chances of both of us getting in there is incredibly low, and neither of us really wants to go to college so close to home. They don't have a cartooning major for you, and I want to go to a bigger school. Candice got in at Mizzou too, and she's asked me to be her roommate. I'm really excited about going there, Chris."

"It sounds like you are excited about leaving me here."

"You know it's not like that. You won't be here either. You know that. You have your life to live too. I love you, Chris, but I just don't see how it is going to work for us. You are going to get into Ringling and become the next great cartoon artist at Pixar and will forget all about me."

Christopher's heart stopped beating, or it may as well have. He didn't have any idea what to say, but he knew he needed to change her mind. "Do you even realize how difficult it is to get on with Pixar? Everybody who has ever doodled on a math test wants to work there, and a lot of them are much more talented than I am. I won't leave you, Jen. We can figure this out."

"You're kidding, right? You have put your heart and soul into your portfolio, and it is incredible. It looks like a veteran animator's, not some high school kid's. You have created your own characters and videos and everything. You'll get in at Ringling and move to Florida, and you'll be successful—I just know it."

"All the success in the world won't matter if we aren't together, Jen." Christopher's eyes started to tear up. "Why do I feel like when you walk out of that door, it will be for the last time?"

"I'm sorry, Chris. I do love you, and I always will, but I prayed about it all night and I know in my heart what I need to do." She straightened the picture on the wall by the door that was taken several months earlier at a go-cart track in downtown

Branson. The couple smiling for the camera appeared to be so happy together, and Christopher hoped with all of his might that the memory of that day would be enough to make her reconsider.

His hopes were dashed when she wiped her eyes and opened the door to leave without even looking back at the devastated boy behind her. Christopher stared at the closed door for a full seven minutes before realizing that it might actually be over.

Chapter 3

"Come on, it'll be fun!" Adam pleaded.

"Look at that thing. How can you even think that would be fun?" Eve sighed.

"You know we can't die, hon. What is there to worry about?"

"Nobody said we can't get hurt. That thing is nuts, but I'll do it if it will make you happy. Otherwise, I may have to hear about this for decades."

The first couple stood on the boardwalk staring at the Eilat slingshot ride. It is essentially a steel-framed glass-like bubble with two padded, restrained seats hooked to a giant bungee cord on each side. When occupants are strapped in, it pulls the ball all the way back and shoots it like a slingshot into the heavens, roughly 230 feet at about 112 miles per hour. Then it springs back and takes a second, less powerful launch, shooting forward again and again until the momentum slows and the ride operator reclaims it to reset the attraction for the next set of passengers. Of course, when riders disembark, they are forced to go through a gift shop area with pictures of their terrified faces projected onto the wall in front of them for purchase. In case the visitor is able to resist the impulsive purchase of their documented experience, they are offered other ways to remember with the obligatory items, like Eilat slingshot T-shirts, souvenir key chains, and refrigerator magnets.

While Adam was wide-eyed and visibly excited, Eve had resigned herself to be strapped into the seat to get it over with. Side by side they walked up, handed their tickets to the operator, and climbed in. It seemed like an eternity from the time the ball was pulled back into position and Eve was ready until it launched into space. But when she willed her squinched eyes to open, the breathtaking view took her mind off throwing up, and the two bounced back and forth to a stop without incident.

The ride operator opened the hatch on the sphere and helped Eve out. As soon as they were clear of danger, Adam pulled Eve close to him and whispered into her hair, "That was so fun!" He squealed loud enough for only her to hear his unbridled enthusiasm.

"Yeah. Fun," Eve tried to agree. Before they were herded through the gift shop, they saw a familiar face smiling at them from the other side of the safety fence that surrounded the ride's loading and unloading platform.

"Hey, you two."

"Hi, Michael," Eve said as she and her husband approached the divided area.

"Is that thing fun? It looks insane to me."

"Yes! It's a blast," Adam answered. "You should definitely try it."

"It's a bit nuts," Eve answered, rolling her eyes at her husband.

Michael laughed. "Your name is Eve, right?" She nodded. "I'm sorry, I didn't catch your name today," Michael said, shifting his attention to her right.

"Adam. I understand. It is hard to notice me when I'm beside this one in a bathing suit."

"No, man, I didn't mean anything like that. Wait, Adam and Eve? That's funny."

Adam nodded, "Yeah. We get that a lot."

Eve decided to change the subject, "We didn't know you were coming up here tonight. We could have ridden together."

"To be honest, I didn't know either. I just kept having this feeling that I needed to be here. I went back to my room and was going to hang out there all night because I was pretty bummed. I didn't feel like doing much, but I just kept feeling like I needed to go to Eilat and find the slingshot ride. So I came here and found you. Weird, huh?"

Adam and Eve looked at each other and grinned. "Very," Adam said.

Eve knew that neither of them thought it was weird. They had plenty of experience with divine intervention and knew to entertain it whenever it was recognized.

Adam took his wife's hand and asked, "You hungry? We were just getting ready to go find dinner. Would you like to join us?"

"That would be great," Michael said, pointing at the gift shop.

Adam and Eve understood and left the disembarking area to enter the gift shop from the ride-side, and Michael circled around to enter through the exit. They met up again by the Christmas ornaments with a picture of the Eilat slingshot ride on the side.

Michael continued their conversation as if they hadn't had to momentarily relocate. "I would very much like to get dinner if you're up for that. I'm by myself on this part of the trip and it feels awkward to eat alone. I was on a group tour for ten days through the Holy Land, and I always had someone to eat with. Now that it is over and I am on my own, it's a different story. I had pretty much decided to just get something at a walk-up window and eat at my hotel tonight. The last time I tried to fit in here on my own, it was a disaster. I went to a Burger King after our dive and completely embarrassed myself."

"What could you possibly do in a Burger King to get embarrassed?" Eve inquired as the trio left the gift shop and started strolling down the boardwalk looking for a place to eat dinner.

"I was just so stupid. I ordered a Whopper with cheese, and when the cashier said that I couldn't have that, I went all American on her. I said, 'What do you mean I can't have a Whopper with cheese? This is Burger King. That's what you sell!' Then she very graciously explained to the clueless foreigner that I was trying to order a non-kosher item in Israel. Apparently, by Jewish law, you can't have meat and cheese together. So, I had to be even more American and ask if I could have a slice of cheese on the side. Poor girl just stood there staring at me until I said, 'Fine. I'll have a Whopper and a drink.' She smiled and rang it up, but the people behind me in line all started whispering things. I know I turned red."

"Understandable though. You aren't used to thinking like that." Eve studied the restaurant they were passing by, but it looked very expensive so she kept walking without interrupting the conversation by pointing it out.

"Right! Even the elevators are weird here. Have you noticed the ones that open on their own on the Sabbath so you don't even have to push the button to get on and off? Crazy!"

"They are serious about biblical law here," Adam offered.

"That's Old Testament stuff, though, isn't it?" Michael asked.

"Yeah, but many Jewish people only believe the Old Testament and still try to follow its laws." Adam noticed a group of Israeli men were walking behind them and changed the subject, "When do you have to go home?"

"The day after tomorrow," Michael replied. "Where are you guys from? It is nice to have met someone who speaks English."

"When we leave here, we're going to Branson, Missouri," Adam replied evasively, skirting the issue of not officially having a home. Eve looked curiously at Adam but didn't give away the fact that this was the first time she had heard of their plans for a stateside visit.

"You're kidding, right? Seriously? Branson?" Michael said, astonished.

"Nope. We'll be visiting a friend of ours who lives on Lake Taneycomo."

"Wow! Out of all the places in this world for you to be from. I have a place in Missouri near Table Rock Lake, which feeds into your friend's lake. So the weird continues," Michael marveled.

I have a feeling you are going to be seeing a lot of weird, Eve thought to herself, realizing that God had supplied Adam with their upcoming itinerary in the exact moment it was needed.

"What do you think about this place?" Adam asked, indicating a cozy restaurant with seats both inside and out. "I like those tables overlooking the harbor. Wanna try it?"

Michael glanced over the prices on the menu that were posted near the entrance. "Works for me."

A kind, young, local waitress came to their table and introduced herself. Once everyone had ordered their food and settled into waiting for it to arrive, Eve clasped her hands together in front of her and leaned on her forearms. She looked directly into the American's eyes and said, "Tell us what's going on with you, Michael. Why are you here by yourself, and what is it that is on your mind?"

Michael was caught off guard by the expectancy in Eve's eyes and looked to Adam for support. Adam leaned in close, sat silently and focused his attention solely on Michael. Although it seemed odd to Michael that they were so interested, he shrugged his shoulders and began to describe his situation.

Before long, Adam and Eve were able to start putting together clues that elucidated why they had journeyed all the way to Eilat, Israel.

Chapter 4

The ceiling was spinning. Outside the rain hammered the house, and Christopher knew how the shingles felt. He closed his eyes causing tears to squeeze out from between his lids, but he didn't even bother to wipe them away. His entire life had been planned out for so long, and it was suddenly becoming unraveled. Had Jennifer left him because of the reasons she had given or because she didn't love him anymore? He grabbed his phone and scrolled through messages she had written to him; he clicked on pictures of the two of them smiling and laughing together. No, she loved him. He knew she did, so she must have been honest with him. She had never lied to him before, and he was sure she wasn't lying now. He sat up, wiped the tears from his face, and sighed as he reached for his laptop. *If she is leaving me because I am going to be too far away,* he thought, *I just need to find a way to be closer.* He typed "University of Missouri cartooning" into his computer and read the list of hits. He was mildly interested in an article that detailed Mort Walker's time at Mizzou. The creator of *Beetle Bailey* had made it there, but as impressive as that was, it didn't top what he had found at Ringling College of Art and Design for cartooning.

He tried again and entered "majors at Mizzou." This time he found a bulleted list and immediately went to "Cs" hoping to find cartooning listed there, although he had searched for this very thing not six months earlier. He wasn't surprised to see the list jump from "Business Administration" to "Chemical Engineering." Frustrated, he clicked on the link for the art program, digital storytelling, and film studies and read through each one. Again. He tried to convince himself that Mizzou was where he needed to be and that it was merely a different route to his dream job at Pixar. He even allowed himself to consider that it could be just as fulfilling and effective. He had almost convinced himself when he noticed the dog-eared Ringling College of Art and Design catalog on his nightstand, and his heart sank. The fact that the application deadline had already passed for Mizzou didn't even enter his thoughts.

There was a soft knock at the door. Christopher wiped his face and ran his fingers through his hair before he choked out the word, "Yeah?"

The door opened and Lucy stuck her head in to say something but stopped herself when she saw her brother's face. "What's wrong, Chris?"

"Nothing. What do you want, Luce?"

"Come on, you can tell me. Jen didn't stay very long. Did you two have a fight?"

"No, it's really coming down hard out there, isn't it?" Christopher replied.

"Yeah, newsflash. There's a storm and it's raining. Windy too. Wanna talk about the weather, Chris, or are you going to tell me what's going on?"

Trying desperately to change the subject he said, "Why did you diss Cole earlier?"

"Diss Cole? What are you talking about?" Lucy asked as she found a seat on the bed next to her brother.

"He said you walked right past him and that you didn't even speak to him or smile at him or anything, and now he's all in a funk 'cuz he thinks you're mad at him."

"I haven't even seen Cole for months," Lucy said, trying to think when she may have crossed paths with him. "But even if I did walk by him without saying anything, why would that even matter to him?"

"Come on Luce, you know he's been in love with you since the second grade."

"Seriously? He still thinks he's in love with me? I thought he had gotten over that eons ago."

"Not 'til he dies. At least that's what he says," Christopher said, trying to grin. "Can you at least smile the next time you see him so I don't have to hear about how I turned you against him all summer?"

"I guess, but I still want to know what is wrong with you," Lucy said, staring into his red, puffy eyes.

"I told you. Nothing happened." Chris couldn't really decide how he felt about sharing the news with his sister. On the one hand, if he never told anyone, maybe the problem would go away and he and Jen would be together again. On the other hand, reconciliation didn't appear to be on the table, so maybe it would actually help to talk about it. There was nobody on the planet he would trust more than his sister with something like this, but he couldn't bring himself to face it just yet. Putting his heartbreak into words would be too difficult.

Lucy stared at him without blinking. They both knew she would wait like that until he broke down and fessed up.

"Fine. Jen just broke up with me." The rain seemed to hear his words and pelted the window with increased vigor.

"Why?" Lucy shrieked.

"She thinks we're going to drift apart when we go to college and that the long-distance relationship is too hard." Hearing himself say the words out loud made sense. He didn't like it, but maybe she had a point.

"Lots of people make the long-distance thing work," Lucy said, trying to sound convincing.

"Maybe, but she has a point. Even if we make it through college with me in Florida and her here in Missouri, what then? I want to work for Pixar and, even if I can't get on with them, I will need to be in a city if I want to work in animation. She won't leave Missouri. She doesn't know what she wants to major in, but she knows she wants to live and work here for the rest of her life. She can't imagine leaving Missouri, and I can't imagine staying here. She can't see how it will work, so she ended it now." Even though Chris could appreciate the logic in his words, his heart seemed to break all over again, and the lump in his throat started to burn.

"Maybe she thinks ending it now will make it easier on you both in the fall," Lucy said.

He sighed and wiped a single tear from his eye. "She probably just wants to be free this summer to date other people."

"She's not like that, and you know it, Chris. She's making a mature decision, and she might even be right. You're a great guy, and I know you will meet someone else that you care about even more than you can imagine right now."

Christopher didn't even want to consider that. "I don't want anyone else. I want to marry *her*, Luce."

It was obvious Lucy didn't know what to say to that. Instead of trying, she just put her arms around her brother and pulled him close. She held him there as long as he would allow it. When he pulled away, she kissed him on the top of the head and told him that time eases all pain before she got up to leave his room. "What is your shift tomorrow?" she asked, ready to close the door.

"I have to be there at eight in the morning, but I don't get off 'til six thirty. I have to cover a second shift for a friend."

"Wanna go get a pizza afterward with your sister? I know it's not much of a Saturday night date, but I'd enjoy it."

Chris was touched by her concern. "I guess. My schedule is suddenly open."

At ten minutes to eight the next morning, Christopher stood wide-eyed in the driveway looking at his prized Jeep peeking out from under the tree that used to support his childhood treehouse. The storm didn't appear to have damaged anything else, which just made his bad luck seem worse. His best friend was mad at him, his girlfriend had dumped him, and now his Jeep looked like a hot dog bun. He sighed and went back inside.

Christopher arrived at his job seventeen minutes after eight in his sister's car. He had never been late before and was confident that his boss would understand. Surely he would realize that nobody could have planned for the surprise that he found in his driveway that morning.

"I don't care," his boss screamed at Amber. "This is the fourth time in two weeks you have been late, and I am trying my hardest to run a business here. You have no respect for the rules, and you seem to think that none of them apply to you. I have had enough, Amber. You are fired."

Christopher's pretty little coworker didn't seem a bit fazed when she turned to see him inching his way toward the time clock. "What about your golden boy over there, Mr. Johnson? He's late and I don't see you flying off the handle at him. Where's the fairness there?"

"Christopher has never been late before," the boss said, looking a bit conflicted. "But that's it for you too, Christopher. Both of you get out of here. I want employees around me who respect what this company stands for. Get your things and don't let me see you in here again."

Christopher just stood there and watched his boss stomp off before he had a chance to explain what had happened. If he were honest about it, he would admit he was afraid to even try. He was terrified that, in light of his recent string of bad luck, he would break down in tears in front of his boss. No part-time minimum wage job was worth that. He merely shrugged his shoulders at Amber and turned to leave.

Chapter 5

"So, Michael, let me get this straight," Adam summarized after he blessed the meal. "You call yourself an agnostic because you don't want to say that God doesn't exist, but you have just spent a week exploring the Holy Land because your wife wants you to believe in God."

"That pretty much sums it up," Michael agreed.

"But, is there a reason that it is important enough to her right now that she would be willing to invest the time and the money to send you all the way over here by yourself?" Eve knew Adam was pushing because he wanted to understand.

"Well, I think she wants me to be ready for what's ahead at home. We have two kids, a daughter named Amy who is in her first year of college and a son named Jordan. He's almost eighteen years old now, is a senior in high school, and has DMD: Duchenne muscular dystrophy."

Eve interjected, "Oh, I'm so sorry," but she had to stop herself before revealing what was in her heart. She knew Michael would think that she was merely offering sympathy for having a child with a debilitating disease, but her sentiment was much deeper than that. Ever since that fateful bite of fruit in the Garden of Eden, she felt responsible for every death and malady that has come to each and every one of her descendants. She covered her instinctual response by saying, "That must be difficult for your entire family. I'm not familiar with Duchenne, but I do know that in muscular dystrophy the person's muscles essentially turn to fat, and they progressively lose the use of them."

"That's right," Michael said. "Jordan didn't start walking until he was 17 months old after a therapist started working with him. The doctors in Louisiana, where we were at the time, didn't know much about the disease, and, although we knew things weren't right with our child, we were told we were just being paranoid parents. It was a relief when he was three and was officially diagnosed, but at the same time it was frustrating because there was nothing we could do for him."

Eve's heart was melting. She couldn't imagine the pain this man and his wife had gone through, feeling so thoroughly helpless to protect their son against an unbeatable assailant. She tried, instead, to focus on the boy. "How is he doing now?"

"Really well, if you look at the big picture. He's happy and fun-loving and is succeeding in the top academic classes in his high school. He loves calculus, singing, and video-gaming, but the disease is taking its toll on him. He's already lost the use of his legs and torso, so he can't maneuver into and out of his wheelchair on his own anymore. We can already see subtle deterioration in the use of his arms when he reaches for things or tries to lift them, and we know that it will just get worse from there."

"Is the disease fatal?" Adam asked softly.

"Unfortunately, it is. The diaphragm and the heart are the major issues for patients with Duchenne. Without the diaphragm, they can't breathe and, of course, when the heart gets too weak, it can't sustain life. Fortunately, there's been drastic improvement in home ventilator care, which is helping the kids live longer now. When Jordan was diagnosed, we were told he wouldn't see his eighteenth birthday. Statistics predict a DMD patient might make it to mid- or upper-twenties now."

"That's a wonderful gift of maybe ten more years, but I know it is not nearly what you would like to have," Eve said sadly.

"We are grateful for the extra time with him, but the bottom line is the same. It is a difficult thing to watch your child's body deteriorate in front of you. My wife, Elise, tries to focus on the present, telling herself that every day that he is alive is a small miracle. I try to do that as well, but usually my thoughts drift to the future, and the thought of losing him can be a bit overwhelming. Elise keeps saying that prayer is the answer and that God can take this burden from us, but Christians die all the time. I guess I've resisted taking her view because I feel as if one day, I am going to have to pick up the pieces when everything she is trusting in fails."

Eve was deeply saddened for the unbelieving man sitting in front of her. She knew her Father in heaven was holding Jordan's hand and his mother's, but his father was choosing to remain lost. "So, you decided to come here. Why?"

"Elise sent me to find answers before he turns eighteen. At least that's what she tells everyone. I don't know what questions I am supposed to find answers to, but she keeps saying that I need to find the answers. Elise would have loved to see everything I have seen and to have been here to explain it all to me. But she needs to be there with him, so I'm on my own. I think she hopes I'll come home believing in everything she does, and that I'll be able to accept that one day Jordan will be happy and dancing around heaven and all that."

"Where do you think Jordan will end up, Michael?" Adam pushed.

"In a box. When it's over, it's over. That's what my dad always said, and it's what I've always believed. Live your life to the fullest while you can, because when it's over, it's over. It isn't fair for kids like Jordan, but that's just the way it is. Life sucks for him."

So many responses to Michael's comments ran through Eve's mind, but she felt in her heart that she needed to wait. She was obedient to the internal prompting, gave him her most sympathetic smile, and changed the subject. "Why did you decide to stay after the tour was over? Why didn't you just go home when everyone else did?"

Michael visibly relaxed a bit at the new topic. "We booked with the idea that I was going to do an extension trip to Egypt at the end with some of the group. By the time I got the tickets, I had decided that I shouldn't spend the kind of money that they were going to charge to tour Egypt, and that I'd just find something else to do instead to kill the time. The plane tickets couldn't be changed without a penalty charge, so I'm just hanging out waiting to go home."

"Where do you fly from?" Adam asked.

"Cairo. The rest of the group will be there when they're done touring Egypt, and I'll join them then."

There was an awkward silence with everyone searching for the next topic of conversation. It was Adam who took a stab at it first. "Did you experience anything in the Holy Land that spoke to you?"

Michael felt as if he were about to have a dress rehearsal for the questions he was going to get when he returned home. "Not really. It was a good trip, I guess, and I saw a lot of neat things, but to be honest, since I'm not very familiar with the Bible, I didn't know what they were showing me most of the time."

"I understand that," Eve said. "Recently a young friend of mine tried to explain the world of Pokémon to me. He was enamored with what he was talking about, but all I could do was nod. None of it made any sense to me."

Michael was so relieved. He didn't want to be judged, and he needed to be understood. "Exactly! Everyone was so much more knowledgeable about each place, and, honestly, it was too embarrassing to ask for explanations all the time. So, I just nodded a lot and said 'wow' when everyone else did. I asked a friendly archaeologist a question or two here and there, but he was trying to enjoy the trip with his wife, and it felt intrusive to bother him too much. I tried several times to read the actual accounts in the Bible when we were at a site, but I was rushed and didn't know the backstory, so it didn't help much. I wish I had studied before I came here, or at least had notes on what we were seeing when we were seeing it."

"Didn't you have a guide who explained the sites to the group?" Adam asked with a sadness in his voice that Michael didn't recognize.

"Well, sure, we had guides but they would say, this is where Jesus cried over Jerusalem, or where he wept in the garden, or where he healed the blind man. But our guide assumed that everyone knew each story as well as he did, so I missed a lot. The travel company did provide a couple of sentences about each stop in a journal they gave us, but it was mostly full of blank lines for us to record our thoughts and to jot things down we wanted to remember."

"That's a shame," Eve said. "At least you got to see what the area looks like, though, and if you decide to read the accounts of what happened in the places you were actually standing when you get home, it should make more sense to you then."

"I hadn't thought of that. You're right, that's a good point." Michael pondered this for a moment. "We went to Bethlehem, which is the location of a story I do know about. But it's so touristy and tacky now that it's hard to get excited about what may or may not have happened there."

Adam said, "I understand. It's hard to visualize the Holy Family arriving on a donkey and having to fend for themselves where the animals are housed when you're standing in a marble cathedral with decorations everywhere."

"Yes, that's exactly what I mean. I wish it was still a cave or a barn or something like that. I don't know what I expected, but I couldn't help but feel disappointed when we were there." Michael could hear the negativity in his own voice and didn't like it. "But the archaeologist I told you about kept telling me things I could understand. Like the nilometers in Egypt! It made me wish I had kept the extension trip."

"The nilometers?" Adam questioned.

Michael paused for a moment, as if trying to decide on the best way to explain what the archaeologist had taught him. "Before Jordan was confined to a wheelchair, he was more like a normal kid. We would get him to stand in the doorway on his birthday and put a pencil mark above his head on the frame and label it with the date. That way, we could see how much he had grown from year to year. We did the same thing with Amy."

"I've seen people do that before. It's a wonderful way to remember," Eve commented,

"I agree. Well, the Egyptians did that too. Before the Aswan Dam was built, the people relied heavily on the waters of the Nile for farming and feeding people. Every year they would mark how high the Nile's waters came. If it was very low, farming was more difficult and crops would be scarce causing the price of food to be very high. If the waters were high, the crops could be more easily irrigated and produce would be more plentiful, causing the cost of food to be lower.

"This man was telling me that on a previous trip to Egypt while sailing in a felucca, a local pointed out a post with a mark at a very low point. Historians linked it to the story of Joseph in Egypt during a severe famine. That speaks to me! It's a biblical story and there's physical proof of it today. So, I don't know. Maybe I believe that one."

Adam said, "I think I see, Michael. You are a man of science, and men of science are ones who need to be able to see things first in the physical world to believe."

"Well, yeah. If it can be seen, it can be verified, which is why I was trying to talk the SCUBA guy into taking me to see where Moses crossed the Red Sea. I got excited about some things I saw on the internet about a SCUBA party finding chariot wheels and horse bones near an underwater land bridge through the very deep Gulf of Aqaba. Apparently, that report I read online hasn't been verified, and the location of the actual site is still being debated. The guide explained that over the years there has been a lot of speculation about where the crossing actually happened. It isn't even agreed on whether it occurred across the Sea of Reeds, the Gulf of Suez, or the Gulf of Aqaba. And within each of those bodies of water, the crossing sites have been argued as well. I thought it would be fun to go explore it on my own, but I can't. Which brings me back to what I said when I first saw you getting off of that crazy slingshot ride. I was bummed about plans falling through and didn't really know what to do with the time I have left."

"You said you're flying out of Cairo the day after tomorrow?" Adam asked.

"That's right," Michael said after swallowing the last mouthful of his dinner and wiping his mouth with his napkin.

"Any idea what you are going to do?" Eve asked.

"Not a clue," Michael admitted.

"We are planning on visiting the new Egyptian museum," Adam said and Eve smiled at the news. "Do you have any interest in that?"

"Absolutely! I heard that thing covers 120 acres or something like that. I saw it on the itinerary for the extension, but I forgot all about it. I don't think it's too far from the airport, so that would work out great for me. Are you guys flying out of Cairo as well?"

"To be honest, we haven't gotten our tickets yet, but Cairo's airport is as good as any. Heading that way tomorrow works for us," Adam said. "Besides, I don't know if you are aware of it or not, but right now you are on the east side of the Sinai Peninsula and to get to Cairo to catch your flight, you need to cut across 265 miles of territory that is currently hostile toward Americans. The busload of Americans that made up your group would most likely have been okay, but since you're traveling on your own, you could be in danger. I think it would be in your best interest to travel with us."

"Didn't you guys say you are Americans also?" Michael asked, never before considering this.

"We didn't really say," Eve stated.

Adam interrupted her, "But we don't stand out like you do. Our skin color and hair color passes as Middle Eastern, but your American features would be noticed in a crowd. Let us join you. Three are safer than one."

Chapter 6

Sitting in his wheelchair in the U.S. government class, Jordan listened to the teacher drone on and on about the similarities and differences between the Senate and the House of Representatives. His mind started to wander, and his eyes fixed on the new girl in the row next to him. Everybody except the teacher was aware of the teasing the girl had received since she transferred to Jordan's school. It bothered him, but he hadn't done anything about it. He looked at her tattered shoes and wondered when was the last time she had a decent hair cut or a new book bag. Her clothes were clean but not fashionable, and he couldn't help but wonder what her home life was like.

"Okay, you guys. Pick up the sheet and go ahead and start. You may move where you need to in order to work with your partner," the teacher instructed.

Jordan snapped to attention and looked at Christopher for direction. "Hey man, I was zoning. What are we supposed to do?"

Christopher smiled at his friend and filled him in. "Wanna work together?"

"You know I would, but not this time, if it's okay with you."

Christopher surveyed the room and saw a friend who needed a partner and nodded, "No problem. I'm going over there."

Jordan nodded at Christopher and maneuvered his wheelchair to get as close as he could to the new girl. She had her head down and seemed to be intent on becoming invisible.

Jordan couldn't help but smile—not because her pain made him happy, but because he could connect with this hurting person in a way that could make a difference. He remembered what it was like when he first moved to the school and was directed to work with a partner in a class full of bullies. Christopher had been the one to approach him that day, even when both boys knew manipulating a microscope on a tall, hard-to-reach table would be a challenge for a kid in a wheelchair.

Jordan looked at his service dog, Penny, who was waiting for instruction. He smiled at the dog and strained to reach out far enough to tap the new girl's desk. "Excuse me, Alicia is it?"

The new girl looked up, surprised to see Jordan smiling from his wheelchair.

"Hey, I'm Jordan. Wanna work on this thing with me?"

The girl looked around to see if anyone was watching her. Nobody seemed to be paying any attention, so she looked back at the boy in front of her. "Uh, sure." She stared at him a little longer than most people would feel was appropriate.

"Yeah, I know. I'm short. If you stood me up, I think I may clear four foot six by now. I haven't checked lately."

Alicia looked as if she couldn't decide whether to laugh or grunt. The result was a sort of a snort in response to his joke. Jordan smiled and motioned to Penny. The dog went to Alicia and rested her head on the girl's lap. Alicia appeared to relax a little and giggled softly as she petted the dog on the head. After briefly bonding with the animal, she got up and moved her desk so that she and Jordan could work together more easily.

After they completed the group activity, Jordan smiled warmly at his new friend, and he and Penny went back to their area of the room. From his position behind Alicia, the new girl seemed to sit a little straighter and taller in her chair. He smiled and told himself that he was going to make a conscious effort to connect with her whenever he could. *Everybody needs a friend,* he thought to himself. A few minutes later he noticed that Penny had made her way back to Alicia and was enjoying a neck scratch from the new classmate. Jordan smiled to himself and tried to focus on the U.S. government for the rest of the period.

When the class was over, people packed their things while the afternoon announcements blared over the loudspeaker. Jordan pushed the forward button on the hand controls of his wheelchair and inched close enough to Christopher to talk undetected. "I didn't think Friday would ever get here. You still going tonight?"

"Yeah," his friend whispered back. "I have to run home and get Lucy as soon as the bell rings. My Jeep is still in the shop, so I have her car. She also needs me to help her bring all of the table decorations that she made for Mrs. Hopkins."

"Right. I forgot about that. Well, my mom can't pick me up after school today because she's working late, so she's given me permission to drive this chariot across the street to the church on my own."

"Free man, strolling around town, huh?"

"Shut up," Jordan laughed. The truth was that on rare occasions his mother allowed him to wander around on his own in his new top-of-the-line wheelchair. It was among his favorite moments of life. For a while at least, he felt free and in control of what he wanted to do. "You're gonna bring me some nuggets, right?"

"Are your parents coming to the dinner?"

"Mom is. Dad's still in Israel. Why?"

"I just don't want your mom mad at me again for ruining your dinner with junk food. She'll fuss. Again! We're eating at six o'clock. You can't wait three hours?

"Come on man, I'm hungry."

"Fine," Christopher sighed as he stood up and circled around behind his friend's wheelchair to shove his binder in his backpack for him. "Lucy and I will bring your highness some nuggets to the church. We should be there by four o'clock."

Jordan saw the teacher glaring at him with a teacher face that plainly said not to talk during the announcements, so he just looked up at his friend shoving his pencil in the side pocket and nodded his approval. As soon as the bell rang, Jordan waited for all of the other students to leave the room so that he wouldn't be in anyone's way. He waved good-bye to Alicia as she left the room and hooked Penny's leash to his arm rest before telling his government teacher to have a nice weekend. He maneuvered his machine and dog skillfully through the classroom door and felt great to be done with another week of school.

Before heading across the street to the church, Jordan socialized briefly with friends through the upstairs and downstairs hallways offering his weekend best wishes on his way to the nurse's office. He passed the principal, who appeared to be heading for the door to leave.

"You have big plans this weekend, Jordan?" the kind man asked.

"You know it! I have a dance tonight after church," the boy responded.

"Have a great time, son. Enjoy your entire weekend. See you bright and early on Monday with that calculus homework finished, right?"

"Yes, sir. Of course." Jordan sighed. He hated calculus homework over the weekend.

The principal gave Penny a pat on her head, and they parted ways where the hallways intersected. Jordan slowed when he was close to the nurse's office and gave a verbal command to persuade Penny to push the door open. She tried to push it open with her nose and when that didn't work, she reared up on both hind legs and placed her front paws on the door to push, but it wouldn't budge. Jordan had already noticed that the door had been pulled shut, but he knew from experience that Penny had her own ways of doing things. It was almost as if she had a checklist to run through, and if he tried to get her to skip a step, she would get confused, so he waited. After the second attempt didn't work, she looked to Jordan for direction. Since the door handle was a lever and not a knob, it needed only to rotate downward for the door to open if it wasn't locked. Jordan said patiently, "Up," and Penny reared up to place her front paws on the handle and pulled it downward. The door came unlatched and she pushed it open further with her nose. Proud of herself, she turned to look at her boy for praise and attention.

"Good girl!" Jordan said to the dog, smiling at her accomplishment. "I wonder where Mrs. Steadman is. She isn't supposed to leave until after the buses go and I've signed out," he said audibly to the disinterested dog.

He drove the chair into the office and looked around. Without the nurse's help, there was nothing he could do, so he pulled his phone out and started playing Happy Glass, trying to fill the sad container with water. He had been stuck on the same level for a couple of days but was determined to figure it out without help. After several attempts, Mrs. Steadman came in and interrupted his train of thought.

"Sorry I made you wait, Jordan. I had a problem I needed to deal with." She twisted the cap off of a new bottle of water and held it out for him. "Not going home after school today?" she asked as she watched him shove the phone back into the case strapped to the arm of his wheelchair and finally accepted the water bottle. She handed him a fistful of pills in a little cup and he dumped a few into his hand and shoveled them into his mouth. He wiped his lower lip before responding. "No, there's a big thing at the church tonight, so Mom gave my aide the night off, and I'm going over there by myself now." He dumped the rest of the pills into his hand.

"Friends meeting you?" Mrs. Steadman asked as she took the empty pill cup and the half-full water bottle back from her patient. She unhooked him from the straps on the chair as he responded.

"You know it! Everybody's going." Jordan said. "It should be fun. There's a social hour, a service, a dinner, and a dance."

"Ah, to be young again," Mrs. Steadman sighed wistfully.

After he finished in the bathroom, the nurse helped get him situated back in his chair. "Your seatbelt fell through again," she said as she searched for the strap. "One of these days I'm going to figure out what to do to keep that from happening." She got one end threaded through under the arm rest and put it gingerly on his lap before she circled the chair to search for the other end. Just as she freed it, the phone rang. She gently laid the second half of the buckle on his lap and told him to fasten it while she answered the call. He would have followed her instructions and latched the buckle if he hadn't been interrupted and forgot all about it.

"Hey!" he sang out. "Good to see you again, Alicia."

The shy new girl he had befriended not even an hour before was standing in the doorway of the nurse's office. "Hi," she said, smiling back at him.

"Mrs. Steadman, have you met Alicia?" Jordan asked the nurse when she hung up the phone.

"Yes, I have. What can I do for you, Alicia?"

There was an awkward moment where it seemed as if Alicia wanted to answer the nurse's question, but she remained silent and simply averted her attention to look at the floor. Jordan couldn't help but feel that his presence was making his new friend uncomfortable, so he interjected, "Let us get out of your way. Bye, Mrs. Steadman. See you Monday. Bye Alicia. Have a great weekend. Come on, Penny."

Jordan maneuvered the chair out of the office and continued on his way without ever fastening his seatbelt and remaining completely unaware of the oversight.

The boy in his chair and his faithful dog headed to the front doors on their way to the church. To get there, the duo needed to travel to the far end of the parking lot, where they could cross the street with the help of the crossing guard, and then turn left onto the sidewalk using the bicycle ramp. Once on the sidewalk it was about a quarter of a mile journey to where they would turn right and enter the church's parking lot.

As Jordan expected, the crossing guard was finishing up his afternoon shift but hadn't abandoned his post yet. All of the buses had left the school, and the influx of parents picking up students had given way to the mass exodus of carloads of new drivers heading to greener pastures for the weekend. The man in the yellow vest saw Jordan and Penny approaching, and when they reached the crosswalk, he smiled at them and stopped the traffic so that they could cross.

"Have a great weekend, Mr. Moss," Jordan said as he passed his school's retired resource officer.

"Thank you, son. You too," the man replied.

Penny's leash was in Jordan's left hand, and she trotted along beside the wheelchair as they continued to cross the street.

Jordan's right hand was on the controls. As he approached the bike ramp, his attention was focused on positioning his wheels correctly to steer the chair onto the sidewalk. Trying to be careful, Jordan slowed momentarily but Penny didn't. She knew where she was going and that she needed to get out of the street, so she jumped onto the curb and headed to the left. The usually slack leash quickly tightened and slipped from Jordan's grip when the wheelchair wasn't yet in position to turn. Terrified that Penny was loose and in possible danger, Jordan reacted by turning too sharply. His front right wheel was safely on the ramp, but the left one hit the edge of the curb and his momentum was interrupted. The chair lurched forward, jolting Jordan from his unbelted position, flinging him onto the sidewalk.

Jordan let out a guttural moan after he landed facedown on the concrete walk, and the wheelchair clanked and bounced its way to a stop. Penny was immediately by the boy's side, offering her support.

"Get help," he said feebly to his canine friend.

Penny immediately turned to alert the crossing guard but ultimately remained standing where she was when she saw that he was already scurrying over to help and had motioned for her to stay.

"Jordan, are you okay?" he yelled. "I can't get to you right now. Just hold on a minute."

The crossing guard waited for a response from Jordan before returning his attention to the stopped traffic coming from all directions. He motioned to the drivers at the front of each line to wait and pulled his phone out of his pocket to call for help. A teenage girl from one of the cars jumped out and ran to his side. "I'll stay with him, Mr. Moss," she said.

The girl knelt beside Jordan and asked softly, "Hey, buddy. Are you okay? It's Tracey."

"No," Jordan managed to say. His right arm was pinned beneath his body, so he couldn't push himself up, and his cheek was pressed against the sidewalk. "My leg really hurts," he finally managed. "Please don't try to move me."

"Okay," Tracey responded. "I won't. I'll just sit here with you, if that's okay."

"Sure," Jordan said, trying to sound jovial and unconcerned, though he couldn't pull it off.

Tracey rubbed his back and said, "I think Mossy called an ambulance for you. Want me to call your mom?"

"Yeah," Jordan said, starting to panic as the pain in his leg set in. He willed himself not to cry, but it was tough to do. He tried, instead, to concentrate on Penny, who had snuggled up beside him. People started to gather on the sidewalk, but the crossing guard was adamant that they kept their distance, so they watched and whispered among themselves.

Mr. Moss split his attention between checking on the trio around the chair, yelling at the nosy passersby, and directing traffic out of the way. Before long an ambulance arrived, and the paramedics swung into action. A nervous new EMT named Susan placed the backboard parallel to Jordan but in front of him.

"We're going to have to flip him over to place him on the board," her mentor said softly.

"I knew that. Sorry," Susan muttered as she quickly lined up the board up behind the patient.

"It's okay. You'll get the hang of it. Let Pat through so we can get him situated."

"How are you doing, buddy?" the paramedic asked softly with his face inches from Jordan's. "My name is Brian. What's your name?"

"Uh, Batman," Jordan tried to joke.

"I know it's embarrassing son, but we all fall down. You are in good hands. Can't you trust us with your name?"

"Yeah, I guess. It's Jordan. Is my dog okay? She was here a little while ago, but I don't know where she went. Her name is Penny."

Brian looked at Susan and jerked his head toward the dog. She nodded her head and rushed over to take possession of the confused service animal.

Brian continued, "Yes sir, Penny is in good hands. My friend Pat is behind you. When you are ready, we're going to lift you onto the board, but before we do, we need to know what is hurting you."

Brian had already begun tenderly running his hand over Jordan's arms and back, applying a little bit of pressure and looking for a response from the boy. So far, he had found nothing of concern.

"Did you hit your head, Jordan?"

"Not hard. It's my leg, man!" Jordan gurgled. "My leg isn't right. I can't feel it, and it really hurts at the same time."

"Your right leg?" Brian surmised.

"Yeah. The other one's okay, I think," Jordan mumbled.

Brian did his best to identify and stabilize potentially injured areas. He strapped on a neck brace before attempting to move Jordan. When he was ready, Brian said, "Okay, Jordan. This may hurt for a bit, but we have to turn you over to get you onto the board so that we can get you into the ambulance. You can trust us. We do this all the time. Do you think you can be brave and let us try to help you?"

"Oh, man, that's gonna hurt!" Jordan whined.

"But it's bound to be better than hanging out in the street, don't you think? Come on Batman. Can you handle it?"

"Yeah. I can handle it," Jordan said between gritted teeth. "Go ahead."

"Are you ready, Pat? Ok, Jordan, here we go."

Jordan tried his hardest to suppress a scream, but he couldn't. Tears filled his eyes, but he refused to cry. After what seemed to be an agonizingly long time, the EMTs fastened him to the backboard and lifted him into the ambulance. He opened his eyes and looked at all the people surrounding the open ambulance door. Their attention appeared to have shifted to the dog and the 700-pound wheelchair. They all stood there for a few minutes with their hands on their hips, trying to figure out what to do.

As if on cue, two women ran up the sidewalk to save the day. Elise and Amy scurried to the open end of the ambulance and tried to see inside before their progress was blocked by those on duty.

"Excuse me, ma'am. Can I help you?" one of the paramedics asked.

"Yes," Elise responded breathlessly. She put her hands on her thighs and bent at the waist for a moment, trying to catch her breath. Before she could respond further, Jordan yelled to the men who had been taking care of him thus far.

"That's my mom and sister!"

Elise nodded while she was still trying to catch her breath. Amy was the one to speak up. "We couldn't get through to you with the traffic backed up, so we parked our van down the street and ran here. I can take care of the wheelchair and the dog, if you'll let Mom ride to the hospital with my brother."

Elise smiled her confirmation and stood up straight. She got the nod from the paramedic and hoisted herself into the back of the ambulance to sit on the bench beside her son.

"What did you do?" she asked when they were finally underway to the emergency room.

"I hit the curb. Penny's leash got away from me, and I jerked to grab it, and I guess the front wheel hit the curb."

"But why did you fall out? That would have jerked you terribly, for sure, but why did you fall out?"

Jordan had been thinking about that and had come to the realization that he had forgotten to buckle himself back in when he left the nurse's office. Telling his mother he had been that careless was not something he looked forward to doing, so he just shrugged his shoulders as if he had no clue. When that motion hurt his neck and he complained, the topic got switched, and at least for the moment he was relieved.

"Ma," Jordan asked softly. "Could you call Christopher for me and tell him that I won't be at the church tonight? He's expecting me to be there, and I don't want him to worry." The hurting boy didn't mention the chicken nuggets he knew he wasn't supposed to have. He was well aware that he would be in enough trouble without adding illegal calories that he didn't even get to enjoy into the mix.

Elise pulled her phone out of her purse and started to search for Christopher's number when it rang in her hand.

Chapter 7

Adam pulled the gas nozzle out of the car and placed it in its holder on the pump. He leaned in through the open window to ask Eve if she wanted anything from inside before they set off.

"I could use a bottle of water," she replied. "Don't you think Michael has been gone too long?" she asked with a tone of concern in her voice.

Adam felt a surge of unrest in his soul. Something didn't feel right. "I'll check on him. Be right back."

Earth's first man glanced around the rental car with what an observer would describe as intentional searching. Everywhere Adam and Eve had ventured since expulsion from their normal existence roughly six thousand years earlier, two angels had traveled with them. Andel's assignment was to watch over Eve and Caleb's was to watch over Adam. The four trusted each other without limitation and often found it amusing to go up against the goons, Damien and Diego, that the evil one would send to thwart whatever the challenge of the day presented. They never had to worry about who would be victorious, but they knew the mortals they dealt with were not as invincible as they were. Sometimes God allowed those they were helping to die or to be injured. The greater purpose behind those events would be revealed later, but they were always heartbreaking to watch in the moment. Adam hoped that this wasn't one of those times, but either way, he needed to find Caleb immediately.

Adam didn't have to search long before he heard, *I'm right here, friend.* The currently invisible Caleb communicated calmly and telepathically to his human companion. *Andel went in with Michael to watch over him. I have to tell you, though, that Damien and Diego know we are here, and they have been inciting the locals against us.*

Adam responded silently. *Eve and I expected that to happen. As I'm sure you are aware, we talked at length last night about whether we are actually a benefit or a liability for Michael in this part of the world. Ultimately, though, we decided our Father is greater than the Enemy and he wants to deliver us all through this trial.*

Our thoughts exactly, my friend, but you need to be alert. Damien and Diego are coming for you.

Adam hurried to search for Michael with a new urgency. He heard some commotion coming from the bathroom and entered cautiously. Immediately, he saw Eve's angelic companion Andel, appearing in human form as a local bedouin, standing between a terrified Michael and two young ISIS members with white-knuckled grips on the stocks of their machine guns. The local men were shouting in Arabic at Andel and pointing at Michael who was trying to shrink out of sight behind the partition between the urinals and the single stall.

Adam felt the weight of the door that he was holding open lessen and turned to see who else was coming to join the chaos. He suppressed the urge to laugh when he found himself face to face with the usually jovial Caleb, donning the seriously perturbed look of an overworked Egyptian police officer who appeared irritated to be in a position to save an ignorant American from his country's current threat to the ruse of hospitality.

"What's going on here?" Caleb asked in loud authoritative Arabic.

"Nothing we need your help with," one of the militants responded.

"Come on, son, I think it would be best to leave now," Officer Caleb said to Michael in passable English. "Move aside and let him through."

The ISIS boys parted to let Michael through, but it was obvious to everyone present that they were not going to let this easy prey get away so effortlessly.

Adam and Michael ran to the car and jumped in. Eve was reading the GPS directions on her phone to get an idea of what lay ahead when Adam cranked the engine and sped off. "Where's my bottle of water?" she asked.

"Sorry, hon. I got sidetracked. We'll stop again soon and get some."

"Sidetracked? You call that sidetracked?" Michael shrieked. "All I can say is that I'm glad I used the bathroom before it got crazy in there."

"What do you mean?" Eve asked, turning to look at the scene they had just left.

"I think I was about to get abducted," Michael responded. "Good thing you and that police officer showed up when you did!" he squealed.

"Police officer?"

Adam winked at her and she understood.

"I heard one of them calling someone as we were leaving," Adam said. "We're not done with them, I'm afraid."

"You understood what they were saying?" Michael asked.

Adam decided to be open with Michael. He answered honestly, "Yes, I understood them. They were quarreling over what to do with you. One of them wanted to take you in as a trophy, and the other wanted to kill you."

Adam didn't need Caleb to read Michael's thoughts and relay them to understand his confusion and concern. All the visibly traumatized Michael was able to verbalize, though, was the simple question, "Why?"

Adam, saddened by the age-old conflict, explained. "You stand for everything they hate, and your death or capture could be valuable to their social status. They were young and trying to prove themselves worthy."

"What do I stand for? I'm nothing but a tourist."

"You're an infidel. They hate Americans and Christians."

"But I'm not even a Christian."

"Doesn't matter to them. They see all Americans the same—weak, unworthy infidels."

Adam kept checking his rearview mirror for the unwanted company that he was sure would be arriving soon. Several minutes later, a dingy white pickup truck that had spotlights mounted on the roof sped by them, coming in the opposite direction. As soon as the driver could get a good look at Adam's car, the truck's front end lurched downward indicating the driver had slammed on the brakes. Adam accelerated and passed the truck, noticing the fierce stare from the driver as he went by. He looked in the rearview mirror and saw the back end of the truck fishtail. Its pace decreased, then it spun around, kicking up sand and rocks. When the cloud of dust dissipated, Adam realized that the driver was doing everything he could to close the gap between them. It wasn't long before the truck's grille filled Adam's rearview mirror. He adjusted the mirror and saw the angry face behind the wheel, gritting its teeth.

Michael noticed Adam's reaction and spun around to check the situation for himself. "There's a bunch of them and at least one with a gun!"

One of the men in the truck was fighting hard to remain standing in the bed, his machine gun poised over the cab and aimed at the fleeing intruders. Adam knew as soon as the truck settled in behind them and the hostile gained his balance, they would be in trouble. The first bullet ripped through the trunk and the second shattered the back glass. Adam remained under control, but Michael was hysterical.

The third bullet found its way through the broken back glass and traveled through the middle of the car to shatter the rear-view mirror. The fourth hit the left side of the headrest behind Eve's bowed head, just missing her ear.

Calmly, Eve put her hand on her husband's thigh and started to pray. "Father, we are in need of your guidance, your protection, and your favor. We love you and serve you, and we want to deliver your son Michael home to his family unharmed. We know you promise that when two or more are gathered in your name, that you are there with them, and Father, we are indeed coming to you now in need. We pray that you deliver us from those who are trying to harm us and that you bless them with the good news of your son, so that they too may be saved from an eternity without you. If it is your will that we be taken down, we submit to your higher purpose. But if you see us safely through to our destination, we will be truly grateful. We also ask that you put a hedge of protection around this car and its occupants until we reach a place of safety. All that is ours is yours. We love you and thank you for the opportunity to share your love with our new friend, Michael. In Jesus' holy, unmatched name, amen."

Adam squinted to make out the road ahead but could see nothing. An ominous wave of windblown sand made its way toward the approaching car and soon engulfed them, sandblasting the paint from the car's exterior. Adam slowed because he couldn't see, but he knew the road was straight and virtually empty. So he kept his bearings and listened for promptings from his angel buddies or his Creator. Both, he knew, would protect him. As soon as the sandstorm had moved over them, Eve craned her neck to see the mess they left in their wake. The pursuing truck was sliding out of control on its side, and its occupants were strewn about, some picking themselves up and others writhing in the dirt.

"Praise Jesus," she said. "God is good."

"Amen!" Adam said. "Glad he told us to get the comprehensive insurance."

"You think God did all that?" Michael asked, not believing his own eyes.

"Of course. Don't you?" Eve asked.

"Why would he save us?"

"Because we asked him to," Eve stated simply.

The frustration that Adam had felt the first night they met resurfaced. He tried to keep it out of his voice but was certain he failed. "Michael, think about it. You were outnumbered at the gas station, and a policeman who wanted to help you just happened by at the right time. This car was under attack with no defense possible and nowhere to go. So Eve prayed for help, and a lone sandstorm at precisely the right time takes the aggressors out of the equation. And you question whether God helped us? Why is that so hard for you to believe?"

"Because he has never had any interest in helping me before. I used to pray for Jordan, but nothing ever came of it. I prayed asking for things all the time but never got any of it. Why should he start listening now?"

Typical American logic, Adam thought. *God wants me to have everything I want and to always be happy.* He sighed and tried to enlighten his friend. "Maybe because you were treating the God of the universe like a genie in a bottle. He isn't a wish granter, Michael; he is God. He is in control of everything, and even though he has power over all things, he only wants a relationship with us. He could control that as well, but he chooses for us to have free will. If we seek him, we will find him. If we reject him, we are often left fending for ourselves."

"Wait a minute. You are saying that God acted in response to your prayer? But the gas station happened before your prayer."

Adam was glad for such a clear opportunity to teach Michael about the way God protects his children. He took a deep breath and patiently tried to explain. "He sees all and knows all, Michael, and even if a prayer hasn't been prayed yet, he knows it will be. Beyond that, Eve and I are in constant communication with him, whether we allow you to hear it or not. Just pay attention to him. You will start to see that he orchestrates things around you to encourage you to come to him. Your salvation has to be your decision though, not his."

Michael seemed to dwell on this for a minute. "Eve, why did you pray for the thugs trying to kill us?"

She shrugged her shoulders as if to say, that's what you're supposed to do. "We are told to give praise and thanks in all situations and to pray for others, even those who persecute us. Jesus prayed for the men who crucified him, and we are asked to do the same."

"That's a pretty big ask," Michael commented.

"It certainly is," Adam said. Eve nodded in agreement with one eyebrow raised.

Almost three hours later Adam drove the bullet-ridden, sandblasted rental car into Cairo. Even the Egyptians, who are used to seeing evidence of violence appearing in their city, took notice of the car full of foreigners and the signs of recent conflict. Its occupants looked calm and even content, and that, perhaps, interested the onlookers the most. The trio followed the signs to the Grand Egyptian Museum's parking area, parked, and headed for the entrance.

Michael grabbed Adam's sleeve and jutted his chin in the direction he was looking. Adam followed his gaze and laughed. "Don't be afraid of him, Michael. Armed guards are posted all over tourist locations in Egypt with instructions to protect visitors at all cost. Egypt relies heavily on tourism, and the industry has taken such a serious beating lately that they are serious about protecting you. You're very safe because it is in their best interest to provide you with the best experience possible. They assume you'll likely return home and spread the word about how many interesting artifacts you saw and how safe you felt, and your friends and their friends will all come to Egypt and spread their wealth around. That is their dream and their prayer every night to Allah. At least for now, you're safe." Adam smiled when he could see his new friend relax a little. He knew intuitively that he and Eve were gaining Michael's trust.

By the ticket counter, there was a large banner that boasted the museum's possession of King Tut's chariot. "That should be interesting," Michael said, and the three pushed their way through the turnstile to explore the numerous artifacts of Egyptian history.

Chapter 8

Christopher stopped to get gas before he pulled up to his house and blew the horn for his sister. When he didn't see any movement inside, he put the borrowed car in park and decided to see if he could help hurry things along. Just about the time he got to the front door, it opened and Lucy was on the other side trying to balance too many boxes.

"Here, let me help you with that," he laughed.

As they loaded the trunk with the table decorations, Christopher said, "Lucy don't be mad at me."

"Hmmm. You only say that when you're going to say something that makes me mad at you."

Christopher felt trapped between his best friend and his sister. It was so stupid that there was even issue at all. "Intuitive. Well, yeah. I asked Cole if he wanted to go to this thing with us tonight. He's been so mad at me all week, and I really don't know what else to do to smooth things over with him."

"Why would that make me mad? I like Cole."

"Yeah, but you aren't supposed to know what I told you the other night. Can you be cool if he comes with us? He's playing in the band later, but you know he wouldn't go to the Bible study or the dinner if we didn't take him with us." Christopher realized he was holding his breath until his sister responded.

Lucy laughed. "I promise I won't let him know you told me. It's silly anyway. We've been friends for years."

Relieved, he said, "Okay then. I told him we'd pick him up in a few minutes, and then we have to go by McDonald's to get Jordan some nuggets. Sometimes that kid's such a pain."

"You don't mean that. And anyway, you know you're going to get some nuggets for yourself too."

"Yeah, I am," Christopher admitted. "You mind if I drive? I filled your tank up for you."

Moments later Cole climbed into the back seat and smiled at Lucy. Christopher worried that it might have been a mistake to bring him along when he tried to joke with his friend and got nothing in return. Cole was a lot of things, but quiet on a Friday night was not usually a descriptor.

After riding for several excruciatingly long moments in silence, Christopher was relieved when Lucy tried to break the ice for all of them. "I can't even remember the last time I saw you, Cole. What have you been up to?"

Cole's eyes darted to Christopher and his brow furrowed. Christopher figured he was trying to decide whether he had told her that he was mad because she didn't speak to him a couple of days ago, or that maybe she honestly hadn't seen him and his friend was telling the truth. Chris was relieved when it appeared that he decided to give up and at least pretend to believe them.

"Either working or at school. Nothing much else," he replied simply.

"You still stocking shelves at the grocery store?" Lucy asked.

"Nah. I'm a cashier now. It pays a little better, but I liked not having to deal directly with the people. Some of them are crazy."

"Do you know if they're hiring for the summer? I could use a part-time job."

"I don't know, but I could check. I thought you'd find something in tourist central."

"I do like it downtown better, but the traffic is ridiculous. It got really old last year fighting it every day. I have an application in at both Japanese restaurants since they are off the main drag, but I don't really know what I want to do."

"I can ask and get you an application tomorrow if you really want one," Cole said. Christopher rolled his eyes because of the potential complications of these two being near each other all summer long.

"That'd be great. Thanks," Lucy said as she turned around to face front again.

"Either of you want anything at Mickey D's? We need to hurry. I told Jordan I would be there by four o'clock, and it's almost that now."

Ten short minutes later, the trio arrived at the church from a side street and pulled into the parking lot. "Wonder what's going on down there," Lucy commented as she tried to make sense of the unusually heavy traffic on the street in front of the school so late in the day.

"I don't know," Christopher replied. "Whatever was going on looks like it's clearing up now. He grabbed the sacks of food and looked around for his friend. "I wonder where Jordan is."

"It's pretty hot out here," Lucy offered. "You know that makes him feel queasy. Maybe he's waiting inside." They gathered up the decorations, food and personal items, locked the car, and went into the church.

"What time is it?" Christopher asked again.

"Like a minute later than the last time you asked," Lucy said as she placed the last box of table decorations on the floor by the wall. She could tell Cole was trying to help her but didn't know what he should do.

As if reading his mind, she suggested simply, "Let's take the boxes to the fellowship hall. Maybe Jordan's in there helping set up."

After asking around and looking in all of the usual places, Christopher said, "Something's wrong, you guys. Jordan should be here by now. He should have been here about a half hour ago at the latest, and even if he wasted time getting here, I told him I would have chicken nuggets for him at four o'clock. He would never be this late for chicken nuggets."

"He's only fifteen minutes late, man. Don't freak out," Cole said.

"He got out of school over an hour ago. He should be here by now. Fifteen minutes late is nothing for you or me, but this kid is in a wheelchair, and he's by himself."

"He has Penny," Lucy offered.

"You know what I mean. I'm calling his mom."

Later that night, the teens in the fellowship hall gathered to pray for their friend. Before they adjourned to go to the dance, they made plans to visit Jordan the next day after clearing it with Elise first, of course.

When Christopher and the others arrived at the house, they found a contradiction of sights. The boy they almost never saw out of his wheelchair was bundled up on the couch, looking almost normal since the comforter covered him up. His face was scratched on the right side, and his eye was blackened on that side as well. But the smile on his face was as huge as anyone had ever seen it.

"You'll do anything to get some attention, won't you, bud?" Christopher joked.

"No, seriously, man. You just don't know. Wait till I tell you what happened!" he exclaimed.

Elise came into the room with a plate full of freshly baked chocolate chip cookies for their guests. She heard what Jordan had said and rolled her eyes. "He's been working on his story all day. Last I heard, aliens were responsible for distracting Penny, and the Batmobile whizzed by and knocked the wheelchair onto the curb."

"Mahhhhuuuum," Jordan whined.

"Sorry, dear. Go ahead. Tell them how the spaceship flew overhead and the giant magnets sucked the wheelchair into the air, spun it around, and slammed it back down. I won't get in the way."

Christopher laughed. "He never disappoints. Let's see the damage." He pulled the comforter off of Jordan's legs.

"Hey, man! What if I was naked under there?"

"That would explain why the alien ship threw you back down. Purple and gold cast? I shoulda figured."

"That's right," Jordan exclaimed. "LSU all the way, man."

"Whatever. Got a marker?"

Everyone who stopped by found a spot to sign, but it was Amy's addition that drove Jordan nuts. She wrote something on the bottom of his foot that he couldn't see, and nobody would tell him what it said. The teens got hysterical when he begged for a mirror, and even after he got one, the mystery message was still out of reach. He tried to talk someone into taking a picture of it and showing it to him, but nobody would. There had been many, many times in the history of Jordan's high school career that he had chosen to torment his friends, and they had no recourse whatsoever. You just can't pick on a kid in a wheelchair publicly without looking like a jerk, and he had played that card well and often. But the tables had turned and his friends seemed to be enjoying the upper hand a little more than Jordan liked. The worst part was that his sister had a lot of embarrassing things on him, any of which could have worked their way into his otherwise pleasant day.

Chapter 9

In the Cairo airport Adam, Eve, and Michael found a bank of comfortable chairs next to the windows and waited for their flight to be called. Eve was busy deciding what she wanted to read on the plane. Adam stared out the window, watching planes taking off and landing.

Michael was still talking about the size of the mummies he had seen in the museum. "I read a series of books on Ramses several years ago. It described him as this imposing, powerful warrior, and to see his body there was a strange combination of awe-inspiring and disappointing. I can't wrap my mind around the fact that the little body I saw used to be the intimidating figure of folklore. Were people really that much smaller than us back then?"

Questions like this were difficult for the biblical pair to answer. Of course, they could shed light on things of this nature, but God had not given them permission to reveal their true identities to Michael, so they couldn't appear to be any more knowledgeable than the average person. In addition to that, they would not allow themselves to lie. "Well, think about this Michael," Adam said, looking up from his phone, "Compare the average Indonesian man at about five foot two to the average man from the Netherlands, who is around six feet."

"Why in the world would you know that?" Michael asked.

"Don't let him fool you. He just looked it up on his phone," Eve said. "It's incredible what the Google can tell you these days!"

"Just 'Google,' dear. You're showing your age," Adam laughed, rehashing the inside joke between them.

Eve responded by wrinkling her nose up at him. He smiled and winked back.

"Anyway, the point that I'm making is that there is a difference between people groups when you look at things like height. As long as someone is the most impressive five-foot three-inch person in Indonesia, he would earn a reputation as being invincible at home. But if he were to travel to the Netherlands, he most likely would lose that title. I would be willing to say that among the Egyptians, Ramses was an imposing figure in his day, but maybe compared to what you're used to, not so much. Also, the lack of muscle, flesh, and armor makes a difference, I'm sure."

"I guess. I just can't see that pile of bones fighting a lion with his bare hands, can you?"

Just then the announcement came over the loudspeaker for ticket holders in group three on United Airlines flight 9105 to board the plane. "That's me," Michael said. "I wish we were sitting together."

"I would think you'd be grateful for a break from us," Adam laughed. "We'll see you in Paris. It looks like we have close to a five-hour layover at Charles de Gaulle. Maybe we can hang out together there for a bit."

"Sounds good. I am actually interested in finding out what the group got to see on the extension to the pyramids and the Valley of the Kings. I hope I get to sit beside someone who wants to talk about it."

"Even if they don't want to talk, I'd be willing to bet they have pictures on their phone you can look at," Eve offered.

The travelers split up and Adam and Eve enjoyed an uneventful six-hour flight from Cairo to Paris. Except for their creaky bodies when they arrived, they were well-rested. Especially Eve.

"Your woman is crazy," Michael said to Adam as they made their way to the next gate. *No argument here*, Adam thought. "Slow down!" Michael yelled ahead.

"No, you speed up." Eve said over her shoulder. "Or just sit down and wait for me to get back. Your choice."

Adam chuckled, "Good luck, mate. There's no slowing that one down. She has a keep-up or give-up policy when it comes to exercise."

"You boys are such babies," Eve tossed over her shoulder as she sprinted ahead. "We have to sit on an airplane for ten more hours before we get to Atlanta. I don't know about you, but I need to stretch these legs and get the blood flowing somewhere other than my derriere." They tried to keep up for a little while, but when Michael suggested to Adam that they stop for a beer at a lounge, he could see that he had a comrade.

"You aren't taking the shuttle anywhere, are you?" Adam yelled ahead, slowing a little.

"No. I'll loop around in a while and find you two. No worries." Eve sped off shifting her backpack with a quick little hip jump-jerk.

"Man, she is something else," Michael said.

"No argument here," Adam replied, out loud this time. "What do you have in mind?"

"I don't know, but I feel the need to indulge in an overpriced beverage. Want to join me?"

Adam nodded.

Michael got situated in his tall chair and teased Adam again for getting water in a bar. For the first time since they met, both men stared off into the distance in the awkward silence that two people just getting to know each other sometimes face. Each was searching for something to talk about, but neither could decide on a topic of conversation, so they sat in silence.

After a little while, a family of four tried to squeeze by their table, knocking it several times. The little girl clutched a stuffed animal and pulled a tiny colorful suitcase, the mother carried a sleeping baby, and the father was attempting to herd, carry, and balance all at the same time. On his head sat a small circular yarmulke.

"That family is Jewish, I suppose," Michael commented, noting the skullcap.

"It appears so," Adam responded, smiling to himself and giving internal thanks to his Father in heaven for the prompting. "You know, God knows you are struggling with your faith, and he may very well have led that family into your view for just that reason."

"What on earth could you possibly mean by that?" Michael snorted. "They just want to eat and wait for their flight."

"Sure, sure. But why here? This isn't exactly a family restaurant that would be chosen by a conservative Jewish father with a wife and young children."

"Okay, so it's a weird choice for them. But what would God be telling me by sending the family into my field of vision?"

"I think he's giving us something to talk about, and I would be disobedient if I let this opportunity pass. So what do you say? Would you like to hear what I think he may want you to know?"

"Sure, I guess," Michael responded with his eyebrows shoved together.

Adam started with a satisfied grin on his face, "If I were undecided about where to put my faith, I would take a serious look at the Jewish people. Simply, their existence would blow the mind of anyone looking at the facts. They started as a simple promise to one old man and many, many civilizations, nations, and empires have tried to destroy them. But they are still here and as strong as ever."

Adam smiled to himself as he watched his new friend. Michael had already shifted in his seat twice and had glanced up at people strolling by on their way to catch connecting flights. He sent a small prayer to his Father in heaven to help this lost soul concentrate on what he was trying to tell him.

"If you recall, the childless Abraham was told in his old age that he would be the father of many nations. Not understanding how that could possibly happen with his seventy-five-year-old wife, he got impatient and took matters into his own hands by having a child with his wife's handmaiden, Hagar. The descendants of that child, Ishmael, are the ones who have been trying to wipe the Israelites out since they first appeared, just like God said they would. And they tried to wipe you out too, I might add."

Michael snorted and rolled his eyes, but he appeared to be listening more intently at least.

"The child that Abraham's wife Sarah eventually bore when she was about ninety years old was Isaac, and through him, God's covenant came to the Jewish people. God promised to protect them and to provide for them, and he has been true to that promise, which is a rich history lesson. Think about it. You have a tiny group of people who start with the birth of one small boy to one old couple. Throughout time, their small family became a mighty tribe. They flourished and multiplied and spread across the known world, but even with the threat of annihilation and intermarrying and plots to assassinate them, they are still around. Many have tried to wipe them out and all have been unsuccessful."

Adam typed a search into his phone and pulled up the list for him to see. "Go ahead, read this list of people who have tried in vain to eliminate the Jews from the planet."

Michael read the list out loud, "The ancient Egyptians, the Philistines, the Assyrian Empire, the Babylonian Empire, the Persian Empire, the Greek Empire, the Roman Empire, the Byzantine Empire, the Crusaders, the Spanish Empire, Nazi Germany, and the Soviet Union. Wow! Hey, Iran is listed too at the bottom of the screen, but the dates aren't there like is written by all the others. It just has dashes."

"That's because the Iranians are still trying to get rid of the Jewish people, but they won't succeed. None of the others did, and they won't either. Our God is an awesome God. He keeps his promises and protects his people. It's incredible if you think about what they have gone up against, but God keeps his word and protects his children. Why wouldn't you want to be one of them?"

"What do you mean? Become Jewish? I can't change my lineage."

Adam smiled warmly. "No, I don't mean you should become Jewish. I just meant that you can be grafted into his family, if you choose to be. Originally, salvation was only offered to the Jewish people, but when they rejected the gift, he opened it up to all Gentiles who believe. I guess in a way the majority of people today should be grateful for those who have refused a spot at the table so that there is room for everybody else. But we are reminded in Romans 11 that the Jewish people are the apple of God's eye and that he's waiting and hoping for as many of them to turn to him as possible. Gentiles have a place with him in eternity, but it is important to remember that they are only guests. This gift is offered exclusively to those who believe and live a life that shows commitment to that belief."

"You really believe all that? Isn't the Bible just an archaic book of old stories about old people making ancient sacrifices and stuff?"

"I absolutely do believe it. The Bible is, indeed, an archaic book of old stories, but it is just as alive today as it was when it was written. The amazing story of the Jewish people doesn't end with just knowing that they have existed through difficult circumstances, though." Adam pushed. "The fact that they speak Hebrew is also amazing." Adam nodded in appreciation to the waitress who set an oversized plate full of cheese fries between the men.

"What do you mean by that? Lots of people speak lots of different languages," Michael said weakly. Adam could tell that even he realized he was missing the point.

"Hebrew died out as a language sometime in the second century. With nobody anywhere speaking it, the language should have ceased to exist forever. But it's the language of God's people, and he wouldn't allow that to happen. In 1880, one man and his friends decided to begin using it again and soon thereafter it made a resurgence. Now it is the national language of Israel and of the Jewish people again.

Michael squeezed the ketchup bottle and it made an awful sound, but not much ketchup came out. He shook it and tried again.

Adam watched Michael try to get the last bit of ketchup from the bottle as he considered, once again, the awesomeness of his Creator. After a moment, he continued. "And, that's not the only thing to come back around," Adam said. "The Jewish people were scattered across the globe as a result of their disobedience and God wanted them to all be together in their promised land, so he had that happen as well. If someone not looking at history through the lens of the Bible were to study the Holocaust, they would think that God had taken his hand off of his people, but the reality is quite the opposite."

"Hold on. You're saying God sent the egomaniacal dictator Adolf Hitler to help the Jews?"

"No. I'm saying that God is an expert at turning evil into good. He wanted to honor his promise to Abraham's descendants and to gather his people together after 1,800 years of not having land to call home. Satan knew this and to keep God's plan from happening, he enlisted Hitler's help to try and annihilate the Jews before God could gather them together. The end result of his attempt was to turn the United Nations and world opinion toward establishing a Jewish state."

Michael interrupted, "So you're saying that when Hitler was finished with killing a third of all the Jews in the world, they were together and happy all of a sudden?"

"No. Things like that take time to play out, and it is still in process today. But the global sentiment for a Jewish state to happen was established then. Except, of course, with the Arab nations. They were violently opposed to the idea. In response, five nations brought over twenty million soldiers, planes, tanks and heavy artillery against the less than one million Israelis and their ten thousand rifles." Adam paused a moment to let those statistics sink in before continuing. "Eight months later the Jewish people not only defeated the overwhelming forces, they also gained more land than they originally had. On May 14, 1948, the state of Israel was born, fulfilling prophecies that were previously laughable to the unbeliever."

"I had no idea," Michael sighed.

"God truly has our backs," Adam continued. "A cursory look at Jewish history shows us that he cares about the promises he makes to his people. He wants a close personal relationship with each of us, and through prayer, that can be achieved."

"I don't know. I feel stupid when I try to pray. I feel like I'm just talking to myself," Michael stated simply. He got up from the table and zeroed in on an unused ketchup bottle on a table by the entrance. He felt to see if it was empty, seemed satisfied that it would work, and returned to the cheese fries. Adam waited for him to finish getting situated before continuing.

"Maybe you *are* just talking to yourself, but that doesn't mean that God isn't listening. If you truly want him to respond, you must accept the fact that he is holding up the other end of the conversation. Take our little excitement in the Sinai Peninsula as an example. We prayed and God protected us. You may say that it was merely a coincidence that a freak sandstorm blew in and relieved us of our attackers. But when you look at the big picture and see that earnest prayer always produces results, you will see a pattern emerge."

"All I know is that prayer has never worked for me. Maybe it's like you say, and I haven't had any luck with it because I don't truly believe that anyone is actually listening to my words. Maybe it's because what you said earlier about me treating him like a genie in a bottle and that I don't see any results because I only go to him when I need a miracle or something. I don't know what the issue is, but I do know that I have never had any luck with prayer," Michael said solemnly.

"Have you ever heard of Brother Andrew?"

"No."

"I was reminded of him when we were trying to outrun our aggressors in the Sinai yesterday. Brother Andrew was a normal guy who was open to the idea of a close personal relationship with the Almighty, and he not only listened to God's urging, he also acted upon it with great conviction. He lived in the Netherlands and in 1955 he earned the nickname 'God's Smuggler' when he chose to be responsible for delivering vast quantities of Bibles behind the Iron Curtain during the Cold War. Obviously, this was during a time when he would have been killed if the authorities had found out what he was up to, but that didn't stop him. Guards at border crossings routinely inspected every square inch of cars entering the communist countries and were instructed to keep all religious materials from crossing the border. They would search inside wheel wells and under seat covers, pull up floorboards and pull off door panels on cars before allowing a traveler to cross into communist territory. Brother Andrew would load his car up and drive to the border and wait in line and pray. Each car before and after his was searched thoroughly, but somehow, they never bothered with his car. Time and time again they seemed to ignore Andrew's car, even the time that he intentionally left stacks of Bibles in plain sight when it was his turn to be inspected. He had faith that God would get him through, and he did. So even though the Bible is an old book with old people doing things we don't understand today, there are countless stories of his continued involvement in the lives of those who serve him even now. You experienced one such example yesterday, and you are not alone. Many of his children witness his divine protection every day."

Eve pulled out her chair at the table and sat down. "Thanks," she said as she reached for the water Adam had waiting for her.

"What are you two talking about?" When Adam started to answer, she surveyed the platter and chose a cheese-free fry with a green pepper chunk.

"We were discussing Jewish history and the power of prayer," Adam answered. "See anything interesting on your trip around the terminal?"

Michael laughed, "How could she? The stores were probably a blur as she sailed by them."

"Funny," Eve said. "Not really, but I do love this airport. I remember the first time I was here and saw all of the tubular escalators passing over and under each other. I had never seen such a modern and artistic airport before. It is still fun to see, but not as unusual these days I don't guess."

Chapter 10

"Wassup superheroes?" Jordan said as he rolled into the calculus classroom Monday morning with Penny following closely behind him. "LSU won this weekend. Anybody got anything to say to me?"

"Yeah, LSU sucks, man. They just got lucky," one of his friends responded.

"You're the lucky one. If Mr. Ewell wasn't here, you'd be kibble for my attack dog."

"You wouldn't hurt me, would you Penny?" The dog heard her name and went to collect the affection that she knew was waiting for her.

"You ever figure out what Amy wrote on your cast?" one of his friends asked.

"Yeah. She's so stupid," he responded laughing. "Mom told me after I bugged her all day about it."

"What did it say?" a transfer student whose name Jordan couldn't remember asked.

"It says, 'Don't tell him what this says.' I mean seriously, how stupid is that?" The transfer student giggled, and Jordan got situated in his spot at the free-standing table in the corner of the room.

Polly was at the board drawing her rendition of Super-Calculee—the calculus class's mascot, which resembled a rotated sine curve with a smiling face.

Tracey was at the teacher's desk trying to figure out what she had done wrong on her exam review sheet. Mr. Ewell tried again to explain, "Remember that when you take the derivative you subtract one from the exponent, and when you take the integral you add one. You switched that around and you forgot to add the plus C to the end of your indefinite integration."

Hannah walked in just as the bell rang and, in her sing-song voice said, "Good morning, Mr. Ewell."

The teacher mimicked back, "Good morning, Hannah." He got up from his chair and went to the smartboard to take roll, checking that each student was in the seat corresponding to their picture on the screen.

Jordan whistled and Penny went to see what her human wanted. Jordan gave the dog a rolled-up piece of paper and said, "Teacher."

Obediently, Penny took the paper to the teacher and waited for her head pat. Mr. Ewell obliged, unrolled the flyer, read it, and showed it to the class. "It seems Jordan is having a birthday party at Silver Dollar City on Saturday, and you are all invited."

"You can come too, if you want to Mr. E," Jordan laughed.

"I think I can find something I need to grade," the teacher responded. "Not that I wouldn't love to spend another day this week with you crazy people."

"You taking one of those flyers to the NHS meeting this afternoon, Jordan?" Mike asked.

"Yeah," he replied. "Spread the word. The more the merrier, as long as you all realize I am not paying for anyone to get into the park or provide you with any food, and you all need to bring me presents!"

"We never expected otherwise," Parker and Polly said at the same time.

Christopher entered the room late but gathered the gist of the conversation without having to be filled in. Every year Jordan's parents put on a big show for him somewhere to celebrate another birthday for their son. Everyone knew that his time left to enjoy birthday parties was limited, and they wanted to support their friend. Of course, if you didn't love Star Wars, Batman and Robin, or LSU, you needed to keep it to yourself or the kid would drive you insane until you caved in and professed undying loyalty to the offended party. At any rate, it made buying Jordan birthday presents easy. You just went to the boys' toy section of Walmart and picked one, and if you really wanted something special it was just a quick stop at a comic book store to find the latest episode of Teen Titans, and you were on your way.

Normally Christopher would have been happy about the group plan to celebrate together, but he knew it would be an awkward situation for him. Should he go and risk running into Jennifer, or would she respect the "bro code" and not attend, allowing him time with his friends without her around? He didn't know, but he decided that she was the one who broke it off, so he shouldn't have to be the one to make this sacrifice. He gave his buddy in the chair a thumbs-up, which Jordan knew was a contractual obligation to be there.

The teacher settled the class down and presented the daily dose of challenging equations for the students to solve and, except for Penny, who was gnawing on her foot, everyone had their heads bent over their papers and their pencils moving. Amy, Jordan's older sister, entered the room with a visitor's badge on her shirt. Mr. Ewell acknowledged her with a simple head nod before refocusing on the struggling student in front of him. Amy delivered a package from home to her brother on the far side of the room and headed back to the door. On the way out, she stopped to look over Christopher's shoulder and watched him for a moment.

"I've always loved looking at your funny cartoons," she said softly.

Christopher looked up and saw her smiling at his drawing. "Hey. What are you doing here? Once I graduate, I'm never setting foot in this place again."

"Jordan forgot part of his history project, and Mom asked me to bring it to him before his next class. Whatchya working on?" They both glanced at Mr. Ewell before continuing to whisper.

"Just an idea that I had watching Mr. E solve for x a minute ago. I can't seem to get the faces right though."

"Faces? What kind of face does an x have?"

Mr. Ewell noticed the lingering guest. "Amy, is there anything I can do for you?" he asked.

"No, sir. I'm sorry. I just need another minute—is that okay?"

"Just finish up. We've got a lot to get through today," the tired teacher responded and focused his attention on a student with his hand in the air.

"They can have whatever faces you can dream up, I guess." Christopher continued, whispering and smiling. "You have to capture the observer's heart with your character if it's going to be any good. You know, like the lamp who pounds his way into the i spot in the word Pixar at the beginning of a movie. It's not just a lamp. He has a personality and you like watching him."

"So, what type of personality will those have?"

"Both are the same little guy. In this first one, he's standing up straight like a plus sign. He's respectable and comforting, like the symbol for the Red Cross, but when he loses his balance and falls over like this one here, he looks more like an x, which repels people. But he's the same little guy being viewed positively in one shot and negatively in the other, and I am trying to get his face to show how he's feeling about the perception of others. I wasn't really going for funny on this one. I was trying more for deep."

"Got it. I guess that makes sense. I heard you and Jennifer split up. I know that must be difficult for you, but you never know what's waiting around the corner for you now that you're available."

Christopher looked up at Amy and swallowed hard. He hoped she hadn't noticed. "Uh, I'm not really looking for anything right now."

"That's too bad," Amy said smiling. "You coming to my brother's party?"

"I guess."

Amy just grinned and said, "I like your cartoon." She left the room before Mr. Ewell had to fuss at her again and in her wake, Christopher's insides flipped over.

Chapter 11

"Ooooh, almost!" everyone in the boat yelled to Adam.

"I thought he might have it that time," Eve said to the friends she and Adam were visiting in Missouri.

Ike finished up his conversation, shoved his phone back in the glove box, and stagger-walked to the back of the moving boat to join in the excitement. "What are you guys hoopin' and hollerin' about?"

Greg was the one to answer. "Adam's trying again to touch the water when he cuts."

"I've never understood how anyone can ski on one ski anyway. It seems so awkward with one foot in front of the other one like that." Ike commented. "How close did he get to doing it?"

"Pretty close. It looks like he's going to try it again," Eve said, pointing.

Adam was picking up speed heading toward his left and his audience's right side of the ski boat. He smiled at the gang watching him before he put on his game face and forced himself to concentrate on the task at hand one last time. *All I have to do is touch the water*, he thought. *Piece of cake. I can do this.*

He leaned away from the boat, pushing his back foot against the ski and digging into the water as his upper body started to descend closer to the surface. The spray from his angled ski arced higher into the air the lower his body went until he was well aware of the fact that he was less than an arm's length from his glassy goal. Since he was leaning away from the boat, the taut rope in his boat-side hand allowed his left one to be free. Leaning too much, he learned the first time he tried it, would result in crashing onto the water and performing the dreaded logroll of failure. The challenge his friend Dale had given him months earlier, however, was to keep his body straight and to either lower himself far enough to touch the water with his elbow, or let go of the handle and touch it with his hand no matter how briefly, before righting himself in triumph. Adam had tried several times to touch with his elbow but could never get his body that close to the water. He had recently abandoned that challenge and was currently trying to get his left hand down there without throwing off his balance.

"Looks like he's going for the finger touch," Greg yelled.

The entire boatload of onlookers erupted in hoorays as Adam's fingers sent a small spray of water upward, and he immediately grabbed the handle to pull himself upright. His face was jubilant, but after persevering through several attempts his knees had become rubbery, and his arms were getting tired. He smiled again and did a couple of fist pumps in the air before gesturing with his fingers across his throat that he was ready to drop the line and end his skiing for the day.

Greg slowed the boat and circled around to pick up the tired skier. "Was that phone call you just took the one we were waiting for?" Greg asked Ike, who nodded in return. "What did he say?" Greg asked as he reached for the ski that Adam had hoisted into the air in his direction.

"I've got 'em. Four seats up front if you want them," Ike responded.

Greg beamed, "Eve, you and Adam are in for a real treat!"

"I wanna hear all about it, but hold on 'til the old man gets in here." Eve reached over the back of the boat and flipped the ladder down for Adam to climb up. Once he was situated, she handed him a towel and stared at him with a huge grin on her face.

"What?"

"I guess you'll be sending Dale the proof I have that you did it," Eve said, raising her phone in the air.

"You got a picture of it?" Adam asked excitedly. "You're the best. Thanks, hon."

"I actually got a video so I wouldn't miss the shot. Not only that, Ike has some good news for us," Eve said turning to Isaac for details.

"I just got off the phone with our manager and he's reserved four tickets on the front row for the show tonight, if you guys feel up to it."

"We would love it. That's very generous of you. Thank you!" Adam replied, pulling the upper portion of his wetsuit down and attempting to dry off a bit. "Tell me all about this band of yours."

Greg said, "Hold on just a minute." He inched the throttle down, gently eased the boat into an out-of-the-way cove and cut the engine. Once they were seated and Ike had the attention of everyone in the boat, he began.

"The Crying Rock Band got its name from scripture."

"Luke 19:40," Adam interjected.

"Impressive," Ike responded. "Usually, I have to explain that one."

"I wouldn't mind an explanation," Greg said. "I've always wondered about the name."

"In the nineteenth chapter of Luke, Jesus is riding into Jerusalem on the back of the borrowed donkey on the day that came to be known as Palm Sunday. The crowds were singing his praises, blessing him who came in the name of the Lord and proclaiming him king. The Pharisees didn't understand what kingdom he represented and told Jesus to rebuke the crowds for proclaiming such blasphemies. Jesus replied by saying that if the people were instructed to keep quiet, the rocks themselves would be the ones to cry out in cheers! So, in today's world, while we are told to keep our antiquated beliefs quiet to avoid being ridiculed, the rocks are crying out. Also, we liked the play on words with 'rock band' since we try to keep our music upbeat and fun like classic rock bands did."

"Oh, got it," Greg replied.

"How many are in your band?" Eve asked.

"We have five guys: lead vocals, bass guitar—that's me—acoustic guitar, keyboard, and drums. We booked a venue in town for several months and after that will be heading out on tour. Our second album should be dropping about that time, and we'll be promoting the new songs on the tour. Right now, we're mainly playing the old stuff and throwing in a new song here and there."

"Sounds exciting," Adam said. "Just remember who it is who gave you the opportunity to influence his kingdom. Keep your goals and your eyes on him and your ministry will flourish. You think for one moment that it is the five of you who are in charge of this ministry and your fifteen minutes of fame will be over."

"Adam!" Eve hissed with her eyebrows shoved uncharacteristically together and lips clenched tight.

"Sorry," Adam responded. "I just felt the need to say it. I don't know your guys and don't know your hearts, but I do know his and I have seen many well-intended efforts fail because of personal pride. I didn't mean to offend. I'm just offering my advice."

Ike smiled. "It's a rare gift to have someone tell it like it is so plainly." He paused for a moment as if deep in thought. "You two want to come backstage and join the band after the concert tonight? I think we could all use a pep talk and something tells me you're the man to do it, Adam. To be honest, we're experiencing a few growing pains."

Chapter 12

"We're so glad you could come to our teen-charged weekend celebration," Elise said as she welcomed her husband's new friends Adam and Eve at the door on Friday afternoon. "Did you have any trouble finding the place?"

"No. Michael's directions were perfect, and Siri helped too," Adam stated.

"I don't know what people did before Siri," Elise said, reaching for Eve's bag and closing the door behind them. The first couple looked at each other and smiled.

"Thank you," Eve said as she released her bag and nodded in greeting toward Michael.

"Have you been touring Branson?" Elise asked, feeling a little insecure about how beautiful the woman was. *No wonder he enjoyed wandering around Egypt so much,* she thought to herself.

"No," Eve answered. "We have some friends who live on Lake Taneycomo that we've been visiting for a few days. We went to a concert one night, but mostly we've just been hanging out on the lake. The water's freezing, but our friend had a wetsuit that Adam used to ski."

Elise wasn't sure what to think. She wanted to be hospitable, but she thought the whole situation was odd. Her husband meets this couple and they follow him home? Something was weird about that. "You're not kidding about the water. It isn't that comfortable in August. I can't imagine what it feels like right now!" Elise exclaimed, pulling her eyes away from Eve and sizing up Adam.

Eve touched her husband's bicep. "He's pretty tough. When he decides he wants to do something, a little cold isn't going to stop him. The rest of us just went along for the boat ride." When Eve took Adam's hand into hers. Elise relaxed a little.

"It really was nothing," Adam added. "I took off from the dock, so I was only in the water from the time I stopped skiing until the time I climbed into the boat, and the wetsuit he let me use was so thick I didn't even notice the cold."

Elise shook her head. "I'm surprised he even has the boat in the water this early in the season."

"Yeah. He didn't, but he put it in when we said we could visit," Adam remarked.

"Regardless, you two sound like you're a lot of fun. Michael has told me all about your adventures in Egypt." Elise hadn't missed a single example of the subtle affection that passed back and forth between her guests while they were talking. When she noticed Michael was wearing his ratty old slippers and obviously not trying to impress anyone, Elise started to feel much more at ease.

Michael interrupted. "Honey, let's at least let them get all the way in the house and settled before we overwhelm them." He officially introduced everyone and after hugs all around, he took the overnight bags that their guests had brought with them. "I'll be right back. If you'd like, you can help yourself to some coffee. Elise made a batch of cookies that we won't get a shot at once the kids find them."

When Michael returned to the group, Elise had just started outlining the plans for the weekend. "As soon as school gets out today there's a youth revival at our church. I don't know if you'd be interested in going to that or if you would rather find something in town to do. There's something for literally everyone in Branson, Missouri."

Eve responded, "That's true. Adam and I spent some time here a few summers ago and went to several shows. It was quite entertaining. I think this time, though, we would rather go to the youth rally, if adults are allowed."

"Of course. There will be a lot of adults there. After school lets out, the kids start to gather in the fellowship hall about four o'clock and play games and visit with each other. There's a basketball court, a tetherball pole, a ping pong table, and a pool table. We put out some snacks for them and let them be kids for about an hour. The Bible study portion starts at five o'clock and lasts an hour. I think tonight's focus is on angels." Adam and Eve looked at each other and smiled. "Then at six o'clock there's a covered dish dinner and . . ."

Eve interrupted, "Oh goodness, we didn't bring anything with us."

"Don't worry about that for a second. I've made several dishes that we can take, and we wouldn't dream of asking a guest to bring anything anyway." Eve looked satisfied and Elise continued, "After the dinner, the kids have a dance. We do that the first two Friday nights during the revival month of March, but it honestly isn't much of a dance. Really, the kids just hang out and listen to the praise band. Some of them dance occasionally, but it's more of a social gathering than a dance."

"All of that sounds great," Adam said smiling. "Kids are fun."

"If you say so," Michael laughed. "Then tomorrow we can sleep in a little and have a nice breakfast before we need to leave for Silver Dollar City for Jordan's eighteenth birthday party."

"Michael tells us that this is a momentous birthday," Eve said to Elise.

"Yes, it is. For a long time we never thought we'd see eighteen, but as the years have passed they've learned more about Duchenne. Just the advances in home pulmonary care have allowed us to shift our expectations out about ten years," Elise said.

Michael chimed in, "But we never want to forget how far we've come, and this one and all that follow are to be celebrated."

"Absolutely," Adam exclaimed. "We've never been to Silver Dollar City, but we have seen billboards advertising it."

"It's a theme park with some pretty good rides. It's advertised as an 1880s theme park, so all the employees are in period dress and all the shops have handmade, old fashioned goods. There's a train that circles the park and gets held up and robbed, and the riders witness a shootout. Jordan used to love that when he was smaller."

"Not anymore?" Eve asked.

"It's just tough with the wheelchair," Elise responded. Eve nodded and she continued, "There's a petting zoo and even a vintage wilderness church that was built in 1849 and has morning services."

"I wonder what that would be like," Eve mused.

"No idea. We never seem to be there at the right time. Anyway, we try to go someplace every year that will entertain all of Jordan's friends and give him something to do as well. He can't ride the rides anymore, but there are shops and food and shows."

"And hanging out with the people he cares about. How do you keep it all together?" Eve asked.

"We don't even try. These kids are seniors in high school, so we'll split up once we get inside the gates. The four of us can go where we want while the kids are on their own, and then we will meet somewhere for dinner. That sound okay?"

"Sounds like a lot of fun," Eve said smiling. Adam nodded in agreement. Elise even found herself looking forward to spending time with her guests at the park.

"I hope it will be good. This is the second Friday night of the March revival, but Jordan didn't go last week because of an incident after school. He's pretty excited about going tonight, but it will be an active weekend for him with both a late night tonight and a full day tomorrow. He keeps joking that it's okay—he'll just sleep in on Monday and skip school."

"I could think of worse things," Adam said.

"Me too," Michael agreed. "But don't tell him I said that."

Chapter 13

When the adults got to the church the Bible study was about to start. There were signs showing parents where to take the little ones and which ages were studying which Bible story. Everyone above grade seven was directed to the large fellowship hall. When they entered, Adam and Eve noticed the elaborate decorations that reflected somebody's well-intended efforts. The night's theme was angels, and varying depictions of such carrying harps and sporting over-sized wings hung from the ceiling. Adam could hear his angelic companion Caleb sigh.

Come on pal, you might learn something tonight.

You know what would be more fun? I could appear as a ten-foot-tall chunky baby in a diaper holding Cupid's Valentine bow and arrow.

Yeah, maybe not.

Adam glanced around to see his angelic friend, but both he and Eve's guardian, Andel, were not making their location known. Adam just smiled to himself and found a seat. "This should be fun for our invisible friends," he whispered into Eve's ear.

Eve smiled and raised her chin for Adam to follow her gaze. On the end of the first row was a boy in a wheelchair laughing with several teens. They quieted and grew respectful when the church's pastor stood at the front of the room and cleared his throat.

"Good afternoon, everyone. It's delightful to see so many of you here today. There are several new faces, and we welcome you and hope you enjoy yourselves throughout the evening. This is the second and last Friday of this revival and as you know, we're studying topics that were chosen from a survey we conducted in Sunday school several months ago. Tonight's topic is one of the most requested subjects we received, and it covers the abilities and duties of angels. I have decided to talk about some of the basic things we know about these incredible beings first, then I will share two stories that we are given, one from the Old Testament and one from the New Testament. That will be followed by an activity where we will divide into groups and look up scripture to match an angelic ability with the biblical passage that describes it. The group that correctly identifies the most will win and be entered in the grand prize drawing on the last night of our revival. So, let's get to it."

The preacher plowed through descriptions of angelic abilities and actions found in the Bible, and even Caleb admitted that he was on point for most of it. When he shared Hebrews 13:2, which simply states we may have unknowingly interacted with an angel in our lifetime, Adam couldn't help but think of Michael's reaction to the Egyptian police officer and the bedouin in the bathroom. He had never shown any indication that he considered something supernatural was happening, even though Adam knew it was.

The preacher continued, attempting to educate his audience about the difference between *the* angel of the Lord, or the pre-incarnate Son of God, Jesus Himself, and *an* angel of the Lord, who could be any one of the vast numbers of angels who serve Him. He gave an example of each, starting with the Old

Testament story of the angel of the Lord appearing to Samson's parents and ascending to heaven in the flames of their sacrificial fire in Judges 13:1–23.

"Can you imagine?" the preacher challenged his audience. "You have a visitor standing by the grill in your backyard, and he instantly disappears into the flames and flies into the sky. As a side note before continuing, if you have never read about Samson, I urge you to do that. Read Judges chapters 13 to 16 if you want to see a real-life superhero. There are stories in there about Samson that Stan Lee wished he had made up.

"Story number two takes place in the New Testament. Remember that if we see *an* angel of the Lord, it could be any of the multitude of heavenly hosts. That's what we see in Acts. Follow along on the screen as I read Acts 12:1–19." When he was finished reading, he took off his glasses and stepped back from the podium. "So, here we have a jailbreak scene. I've never understood why some people don't want to read this book. It has everything.

"To sum up this story, Peter is in jail and when an angel comes in, his chains fall off, and none of the sixteen armed guards notice him leave or respond to the gates opening on their own to let him out. My friends," the preacher continued, "if we are right with the One who sends his angels, we are safe in their hands. Let us pray."

After the pastor closed his prayer, he turned the festivities over to one of the churchwomen. She then proceeded to explain the activity, and Eve was pleased to see the enthusiasm of the kids when they were put in groups for a scriptural scavenger hunt. She was a little disappointed later, though, when Jordan chose to eat dinner with his friends instead of with his parents. She felt herself wanting to get to know the boy but didn't want to force herself into his evening, and she knew that if they were supposed to, they would have time together at some point.

"You guys want to hang around for the dance?" Michael asked Adam when they were scouring the dessert table for seconds. "We can go either way, honestly. I enjoy listening to the kids play, but we've got a long day tomorrow."

"Could we stay for just a little while?" Eve asked, reaching for a homemade fruit bar. "I'd like to see Jordan interacting with his friends a little more, if you wouldn't mind."

"Certainly. Would you rather me introduce you to them or just point them out?"

"Pointing is fine," Adam answered. "We don't need to get in their way tonight. Tomorrow we'll have a chance to be more up close and personal at the park."

While the band was warming up and the others were milling around talking to each other, Michael tried to give his new friends the scoop on the teens that surrounded Jordan's life. "You've met our daughter, Amy. She's attending College of the Ozarks here in town and wants to be a high school English teacher. She's talking to another college student named Lucy who attends the University of Missouri, but I don't know what her major is."

"It's nice that the college kids still want to hang out with their high school friends," Eve commented.

"They've all grown up together and are still pretty close. Age doesn't seem to matter a whole lot to the core group. Others drift in and out, but there are four at the center—those two girls and their two brothers, Jordan and Christopher. The two sets of siblings are the same age so our families have been close for as long as we can remember.

"One of Christopher's best friends from elementary school is on the stage. Cole plays the drums and of all of the kids that Jordan hangs out with, he's the only one who has no interest in going to college next year. He works at a grocery store but has dreams of being a musician. He plays for several different praise bands, including this one, but he's just here to play. Jordan says he's a Christian, but as far as I know he's never been very interested in church, and his family life has been challenging. His dad died a few years ago from cancer, and it's just him and his mom now, from what I understand."

"That's always hard to hear. I'd like to talk to him sometime. Is he going to be there tomorrow?" Eve asked.

"You never really know with Cole, but I doubt it. I know he works a lot and is under pressure to provide what he can for their living expenses. His mother is a nurse and does some private care to make extra money, but life is hard for them."

"Are he and Christopher still close?" Adam asked.

"As far as I know, yes. I don't know what will happen in the fall though when Christopher leaves for college."

"What dream is Christopher chasing?" Eve asked.

"He is an amazing cartoon artist and has dreamed for years about working for Pixar. Jordan tells me he has applied to several colleges out of state."

"What about Jordan? What is he planning on doing next year? You said that Cole was the only one in this group not interested in college, but I just assumed Jordan wouldn't be able to attend a university. So, what does college look like for him?"

"He has been looking into online classes on video game design because his real dream is to work for Microsoft. Several years ago, he participated in the Make a Wish Foundation and had an incredible experience. The company granted his request to test prototype video games. He didn't get to meet Bill Gates, but the group of people that dealt with him were truly amazing. They were genuinely interested in his opinions about some of the characters they were developing. He offered such insightful suggestions that they said they would be open to hiring him to provide feedback on games prior to their release, once he finishes high school."

Eve interrupted, "So, the online classes in game design would allow him to move up from consultant once he is able, but he actually has an opportunity to get his foot in the door after high school. That's incredible."

"I know. All of us were ecstatic about the consulting idea at the time it was offered, and from the correspondence that we have been getting, I believe the offer still stands. He'll apply officially once he has his diploma, but we have a signed recommendation letter from the man who was the head of research and development at the time, and we have our fingers crossed that it will work out. If so, he'll be able to stay home and be cared for by his family while he takes classes and earns some money doing what he loves to do. Even if the consulting thing falls through, he has something realistic that he can pursue online. Just having that direction and a plan is huge for him. We feel very blessed by the experience the gamers at Microsoft gave him."

"That's exciting," Adam said.

"It truly is—from every angle. He's excited about the work, and Elise and I are excited that he has found something that he can enjoy while staying here with us for whatever time he has left."

"Absolutely," Eve responded. "It sounds like everything is working out well for all of you."

Elise appeared at Michael's side and took his hand while they turned their attention to the stage to see the frenzied audience watch as the drum solo stole the show. "Cole's quite talented," Adam said. Eve nodded in agreement.

Cole's heart raced. His hands, still clenched around his drumsticks, found rest in his lap as he felt a bead of sweat slide down the side of his face. He looked up from his percussive corner of the stage to see his friends clapping wildly at his efforts. The entire crowd was looking directly at him, but it was Lucy's solitary face that he saw in the sea of people. All he could think of when the lead singer finally said that the band would be taking a short break was perhaps this was the moment he had been waiting for his whole life. Lucy just saw that he could be impressive, and he didn't want to let the opportunity pass.

Cole carefully extricated himself from the equipment, careful not to knock or trip over anything and searched for Lucy once again. The people who had been standing in front of the stage had started to dissipate, wandering back to their seats and to private conversations. Some had started to leave the fellowship hall, at least temporarily, but it seemed every person he passed or made eye contact with offered him praise of some sort. With every backslap, thumbs up, and "Good job, Cole" that he received, his confidence grew, affirming the decision to face his fears head on. He forced himself not to worry about what he was going to say and instead just kept telling himself, *we've been friends forever. It's easy to talk to her. It'll come to me. It's now or never.* He took a deep breath and plowed through the crowd with only one thing on his mind.

Lucy wasn't watching the stage anymore and appeared to have no idea that Cole was making a beeline toward her. She was facing away from him, focused intently on the screen of her cell phone. Cole ran through the scenario in his mind quickly and decided it would be fun to come from behind and surprise her when she was done with her text. He crept into position and waited for his moment, but he couldn't help peeking at the screen over her shoulder while he waited.

Lucy finished typing, *That sounds like fun! I would love to go with you,* and sighed as she let the phone drop to her side. Cole touched her lightly on the shoulder and she spun around to face him. "Cole, hey!" she exclaimed as she pulled him into a bear hug. "You were great up there. You have gotten so good; I had no idea."

Cole's face beamed, but he was at a loss of what to say. He knew she hated when people brag about themselves, but that was the topic of the moment. So he countered with the only other thing he could think of. "It's so great to see you Lucy. You making plans?" He motioned toward her phone to make his meaning clear.

"Oh, that. Yeah. This guy that lives on my hall at school wants to take me to a show downtown, and I said I would go with him. I'm a little worried about it, though, if you want to know the truth. He's been such a good friend for so long, and I hate the idea of messing that up. I know he wants more, and I'm not sure it's a good idea. I'd hate to lose his friendship if things go wrong. You know what I mean?"

Cole didn't know what to say. He wanted to agree with anything she said, but that would give her a reason to turn him down too. He desperately wanted her to rethink the decision about going out with the other guy, but he was too late for that.

He didn't know what to think or to say, and all the hope and excitement he felt just moments earlier slipped away. Finally, he smiled and said, "You don't know that the friendship will be ruined. You might have a great time. Relationships between good friends are the best ones, from what I've heard. I hope you have a great time."

He swallowed hard and turned to leave when she grabbed his arm. "You were great up there, Cole. I am so proud of you."

He nodded and smiled his best smile. "It's great to see you, Lucy."

Chapter 14

Elise swallowed the lump in her throat. She walked with Michael, Amy, Jordan, Adam, and Eve to the park entrance to celebrate her son's eighteenth birthday. Each of them wore matching royal blue T-shirts with Jordan's name arced above the words "Silver Dollar City" and a large number 18 in the middle of the design. Adam carried a box full of new T-shirts for each of the party guests, and Eve bore a bag for gifts from the kids. She would bring the presents to dinner later on. Elise reminded Jordan of the rules they had discussed, and he was doing his best to ignore them all.

Finally, he gave up and said, "I know, Mom, I know. I can't go on any rides, and don't even think about getting out of the chair. I can't go on the chipped paths and have to stay on the pavement. But I can eat stuff, right?"

"Of course you can, dear," Elise replied. "You've got your birthday money, so enjoy your day. And, Amy . . ."

"I know, Mom. I won't leave him unless someone else is with him. He will have someone with him at all times, and yes, both of our ringers are on and turned up." She paused and knew that her mother wanted more. "And I can't let him eat everything he wants or he'll get sick. We'll be fine. Don't worry about us."

Michael put his arm around his wife and squeezed her close in a side hug. "They'll be fine."

The nervous parents, excited teens, and biblical icons continued through the parking lot on their way to the entrance of the theme park where Elise recognized a dozen or so kids waiting for them. They all greeted each other, and the boys stripped down to pull on the birthday shirt they knew from experience would be in the box. The girls, who also remembered Elise's annual obsessive group-identification need, had worn spaghetti-string tank tops to keep from getting too warm with two shirts on. When all gifts were stowed and shirts were donned, Michael took roll.

"I don't see Christopher," Amy commented.

"Or Polly, Tracey, Parker, or Mike," Elise added.

Just then the five arrived together, not really attempting to hurry. "No present yet from me," Christopher said. "I figured I'd let the foodie pick something out from Brown's or from Copper Ridge Candies, or maybe some kettle corn from Frisco's."

"That's cheap, man! I want a duster and a cowboy hat from the leather shop," Jordan joked.

"I'll get you some homemade lye soap if you want to smell like a cowboy," Christopher shot back. Jordan laughed.

Hunter and Chandler spoke up at the same time. "Hey, Mrs. Hammons," they laughed at each other and Hunter finished. "Can we give Jordan our presents now instead of waiting until he opens them all later?"

"I guess, if you boys want to carry it around all day."

"Definitely!" Hunter and Chandler ran to a nearby bush and hauled out a large black trash bag they had stowed there out of sight. "You can only have your present if you promise to wear it all day," Chandler said as Hunter laughed. "But you won't be alone. We'll join you."

Hunter added, "We're at a park dedicated to the late 1800s, and you said you always wanted to be a cowboy, so today is your day." He pulled a used cowboy hat out of the bag and placed it on his own head. He pulled a second used cowboy hat out and placed it on Chandler's head, then he pulled a large wrapped gift box out and handed it to Jordan."

"Gee, I wonder what this could be," Jordan laughed as he ripped the paper off of the package. Inside was a brand-new black Stetson cowboy hat with a braided hatband. Jordan smiled as big as he could and put it on his head. "How do I look?"

"Like John Wayne," Elise said. The teens looked confused.

"That's not the best part," Hunter said. He pulled out three identical small packages and told Jordan to pick. You get whichever one you pick, and we get the other two. Jordan picked one and opened it.

"A handlebar mustache!" Jordan exclaimed.

"Oh, man! I wanted that one," Chandler said as he opened his up. "I got the cowboy one—looks like Sam Elliott."

"That means I have the horseshoe." Hunter said. "Cool!"

Jordan was looking at Chandler's mustache like Penny wanting a treat. "You said you wanted the handlebar? Could we switch? That one is luxurious."

They all pulled the thin paper sheet off of the back of the mustaches and pressed them onto their upper lips. The girls started to whistle, clap, and hoot.

Elise's heart was warmed by the outpouring of affection for her son. As much as she hated for it to end, she knew they needed to move on. "Come on, you guys. I have a group-rate reservation for twenty-three guests, but I need everyone to be present at one time to get in."

Once inside the park, the group voted on the best dinner spot with Crossroad Pizza beating out the Fry Bread Company by a narrow margin. The adults went over the plan to meet and waved good-bye to the high school seniors and Amy, the only college student among the group.

"They'll be fine," Michael whispered in Elise's ear. He knew if he made eye contact with her she would tear up, but he needed to assure her that even though the doctors said that Jordan's eighteenth birthday would never arrive, he would be okay. Although Elise had no way of knowing it, Adam and Eve sent their angels to provide a hedge of supernatural protection around the group.

The blue-clad teens led by the cowboy in the wheelchair made their way around the park, exploring stores and sites together, but splitting off when it was time to get on a roller coaster. When the bulk of the group left to get on a ride, Christopher noticed that Penny wasn't there and commented about it.

"She stayed home. I feel strange without her beside me," Jordan admitted, "but it's nice not having to worry about maneuvering her with the wheelchair around the crowds and obstacles. Aren't you going on rides today?" he asked.

"Nah," Chris answered. "I've been on every ride here tons of times. I just want to hang with you." He glanced at Amy and hoped that Jordan didn't notice. The problem was, he thought, that Jordan did notice and Amy didn't.

"Thanks, man, that's awesome of you. Let's go see what's in the leather shop while we wait," Jordan suggested. Christopher was relieved at the suggestion, and he and Amy fell in line behind the wheelchair as they made their way into the store.

Time seemed to fly by when Christopher got a chance to talk to Amy without anyone else around. At one point, Jordan found something he wanted to buy, and he seized his opportunity by pointing out a hand-carved wooden Indian that stood by the door. Chris guessed it didn't do enough as a conversation piece to disguise their private conversation, however, when Jordan snorted, "Good grief, you two. Give me a break."

"What are you talking about?" Amy asked.

Jordan just rolled his eyes and yelled to Polly, "Hey, wait up. Check this out. I saw at Nellie's over there that they have all kinds of jams. You know what kinds they have?"

"No clue, dude," Polly said.

"I saw frog jam and bear jam and toe jam. I wonder what the ingredient list on those looks like."

"I think I'll stick with the apple butter or the marmalade," Polly replied. "You ever been to the taffy store? My mom wants me to bring her back some."

"Just put it in the bag on the back of my chair with the rest of the stuff you guys want me to carry. I feel like a pack mule," Jordan whined. But Christopher suspected he was enjoying every minute of feeling helpful and part of the group.

"You kinda look like you're riding a pack mule with that hat and crazy thick 'stache!"

"That's right! I'm awesome. Well, feel free to use my saddle bag, damsel in distress," Jordan joked.

A big group came bouncing back from riding the Time Traveler and described the spinning ride as best they could, trying to convince Amy and Christopher to give it a try. Eventually they did, and a small group stayed behind with Jordan until Christopher, Amy, and several repeat riders returned laughing and reliving the fun. Jordan was the first to spot the group sauntering up the narrow walk toward him. Hunter and Chandler, in the front of the pack, looked silly with their fake moustaches and no hats. Jordan held the used Stetsons out for his friends and shook his head at how ridiculous they looked without the complete ensemble. Amy, behind the two disheveled cowboys, seemed to be looking for a boost of energy to make it up the hilly path. Behind her, Christopher appeared to be hopping along the trail with an unusual amount of vigor.

"Hey guys!" Jordan announced after he had delivered the hats to his cowboy friends, "Look what I got that woodshop guy to make me." He held out a wooden Batman symbol and exclaimed, "This baby is going on my wall."

Amy reached for it to inspect her brother's new wall hanging and to offer her supportive opinion. Christopher tried to get excited about the purchase, but he could only look at Amy turning the thing over in her hand. Her hair glistened in the sun, and her enthusiasm for her brother was touching. Only moments before, she had given Christopher that sort of look. Amy's electrifying iron grasp on his arm as the ride ended added to the adventure, terror, and excitement of the roller coaster. *This girl is incredible,* Christopher thought.

Polly interrupted his thoughts when she yelled, "There's the taffy store! Come on—I hear there's a free giveaway and new flavors this year." As the others ran off to investigate the taffy, Christopher and Amy were once again alone with Jordan.

"Hey, Amy?" All three spun around to see who called her. Amy squealed with delight.

"What are you two doing here?" she asked an excited girl and her boyfriend as they approached, hugging each in turn.

"Just hanging out for the day," the girl replied. "Vince is from Virginia, so I'm showing him what Branson has to offer when we have the time to play around. What about you?"

"Today is my brother's eighteenth birthday." Amy said, pointing at the birthday boy. This is Christopher, Jordan's best friend and an amazing cartoonist and roller-coaster partner." She winked at Chris and looked back at the couple. Christopher's heart raced; he had trouble concentrating on her next words. "Guys, this is one of my best friends from school, Rhonda, and her boyfriend, Vince. We're going to get some kettle corn. Want to get some with us?"

Both boys understood the pull of a chance meeting between friends and shook their heads. "We'll be here when you get back. Have fun," Chris said.

Even with Amy running off with friends and leaving him behind for a bit, Christopher couldn't contain himself. He felt as if he were walking on air. He had just been through such a run of bad luck with his job, his Jeep, and losing Jen that he felt nothing could put it all back together. Now he sensed new and exciting possibilities opening, and he felt better than he had in weeks. He wanted to tell somebody, anybody, but he didn't think sharing this renewed excitement with Amy's baby brother on his miracle birthday was wise, so he kept it in. But he had the conscious thought that he wanted to spin around and sing like that crazy nun in the *Sound of Music*. He saw a low rock wall near Jordan and jumped up on it, pretending to be a tightrope artist.

"Be careful," Jordan warned. "It's quite a drop-off on the other side."

Christopher didn't care. He was so happy and excited he just wanted to be a little crazy for a minute. He jogged effortlessly along the wall and was intending to vault off the end. He swung his right foot around to place it in front of his left, but the toe of his sneaker caught on an irregular rock jutting out the side of the wall. He started to pitch forward. His eyes grew big and his hands went forward to catch himself, but there was nothing there to grab. To the right side was a group of young children that he would land on if he fell that way and to the left was a twenty-foot drop onto rocks and split firewood. As he fought with gravity by throwing his arms and upper body in reactive positions, he thought it was the end of a short run of good luck. Just before his momentum took him one way or the other, he was steadied on both sides.

Man, he thought. *I don't know what I did, but that worked!* He regained his composure and jumped down when he saw Amy and her friends returning. He ran his fingers through his hair, took a deep breath, and trotted off to be super-excited about whatever trinket or foodstuff she and her friends had found.

Meanwhile, Jordan sat with his eyes as big as saucers and his mouth hung wide open. "What the heck, man…" he shouted to his friend but then stopped short.

Just a moment earlier, Jordan had spun his electric wheelchair around to see his friend jump onto the rock wall. Feeling a like his mother, he said "Be careful. It's quite a drop-off on the other side." He was concerned for his friend, but what could he do? He couldn't stop him, so he just sat and watched. For a split second, he was jealous of Christopher's ability to jump on a wall and scurry down it so effortlessly. Of course, if he allowed himself to go there, he could be jealous over someone standing and walking to the refrigerator. As he watched Christopher dance along the wall, he saw the unthinkable happen in slow motion. When the toe of Chris's sneaker caught on the protruding rock and threw his balance off, his limbs reacted in an unchoreographed mess of chaotic movement. But then Jordan witnessed something he would never have believed if he hadn't seen it himself.

He saw not one but two angels swoop in on opposite sides of Christopher and hold out their hands to steady his friend on the wall. Christopher regained his balance and hopped down, and when Jordan looked back, one of the angels was gone. The other was still hovering in the air watching him and smiling. Jordan yelled to Christopher, "What the heck, man?" But as he said this, the angel put his finger to his lips and shook his head. It was a secret for only Jordan to know. He freaked out.

"What's wrong with you?" Amy said as she came over to her brother with her friends and Christopher in tow.

"Nothing, uh, ah, I don't know, uh, mmm." Jordan's face was drained white, but nobody seemed to notice that.

"Eloquent," Amy said shaking her head. "You ready to go get your presents and some food? It's about twenty minutes before mom said to meet her, but it'll take every bit of that to get there."

All Jordan could do was to nod and point his chair in the right direction. On the way to the meeting place, he tried to convince himself that he imagined it, and he had not lost his mind.

When they found the adults at the pizza parlor, everybody gathered around the present table. They knew from experience that Jordan would not wait any longer to inspect his loot, so they all found a place to get comfortable before even thinking about getting food. Nobody noticed that the birthday boy was strangely silent until Elise took the Stetson off and put a pointy party hat on him instead. When there was no squeal of disapproval, Michael and Elise looked at each other in confusion. The only reason they had held on to that particular tradition was to make him fuss. They knew he really liked the attention. But fussing made him seem more macho to his friends, so the tradition was continued year after year, and everyone was waiting for the protest.

"What's wrong, honey? Do you feel okay? Did you eat something that is not agreeing with you?" Elise prodded.

"No, uh I'm great. Let's get this show on the road. Take this stupid hat and bring me the biggest present first." Jordan tried to look excited, but his eyes kept darting all over the place looking for something he somehow knew he would never be able to find. He wanted to tell someone what he had seen. But what would it sound like? Not only would he get Christopher in trouble for being careless, he would also embarrass his friend in front of Amy, which was a direct violation of the bro code. Plus—and this was no small thing—an actual angel had told him to keep quiet. What was that all about? He couldn't concentrate on being the center of attention. He needed to stop the world and hop off, just for a moment. He wanted to scream.

Just then he felt a warm, very large calming hand on his shoulder. He turned to see the body to which it was connected, but there was no one there. In his mind, clear as any words he had ever heard spoken in this dimension, he heard, "It's okay, Jordan. We are not here to take you with us. You can stop worrying about that. You are safe. We are here to make sure you have a wonderful eighteenth birthday party and that's it. We are here if you need us, but we are not here to harm you. Do not be afraid. And Monday, if you wish, you may tell your father, Michael, what you saw. He will believe you." And with that, the warm comforting pressure on Jordan's shoulder was gone.

Chapter 15

Michael was running as fast as he could. Trees and flower gardens whizzed by so quickly that he couldn't make out an individual plant by the time he was past it. He knew instinctively that he needed to get out of there as soon as possible. But where was he? The scenery reminded him of the botanical gardens that Elise had tried to convince him would be the most romantic place on the planet to get married, but there were no paved paths like he remembered. He whizzed by natural fountains and waterfalls and fields of flowers before he noticed anyone else there with him. Far ahead, perhaps a half a football field away, two figures ran as fast as Michael. "Hey!" he called out. They did not seem to notice and were apparently focused on the same mission as he was: to get out of there now—wherever "there" was.

As he got closer to the mysterious pair, he noticed that neither wore clothes that he recognized. They seemed to be dressed in animal skins, and they didn't wear shoes. That didn't seem to bother the pair, and they instantly catapulted out of reach like a turbo-boost on a video game. Michael accepted this as easily as he had accepted the directive to get out of this garden at once. When he was close enough to yell at the pair again, a thunderous roar from the heavens stopped him. He couldn't make out what the voice said, but it wasn't happy. Instantly, a throng of angels appeared all around him, some flying, some running, some emitting a brilliant light, and others who resembled superhumans all fleeing the angry roar. As intrigued as Michael was by these powerful beings, he instinctively knew that if they were scrambling to find a way out, it could only mean that his plight was even more critical. He found the courage to dig deeper and run faster, giving it all he had. Once he felt he could go no faster, two angels lifted him by each arm and carried him to a large golden gate where he was set down. He spun around to see the angels who had carried him, and he gasped when he recognized the bedouin and the Egyptian police officer who had helped him a couple of weeks earlier on the Sinai Peninsula. The angelic pair laughed and yelled ahead to the couple dressed in animal skins, who had been running away. Instantly, the two who had been leading the mass exodus turned to wave at Michael and beckoned him to come closer. When Michael was able to focus on the faces, he recognized his friends Adam and Eve. Suddenly awake, he sat up in his bed, soaked with sweat, wide-eyed and confused.

Michael didn't know what to think. He figured that the Bible lesson on angels had combined with his experience in the Sinai and with meeting his new friends, but it felt like it was more than that. It felt real. Maybe it was the cold pizza he had eaten just before bed when Elise wasn't watching. He didn't know, but he was wide awake and antsy. There was no way on earth he was going back to sleep, and he didn't want to disturb Elise. So he got up gingerly and tiptoed out of the room. He decided to go to the kitchen to get some water but noticed light spilling out from under the door to Jordan's room. He changed direction and went to see what was going on with his son.

Jordan was sitting up in bed with his breathing machine face mask in his hand, making Michael feel that his son was excited to have a chance to talk to him. That was a different reaction than he was used to receiving in the middle of the night. To say the least, he was perplexed and approached the side of his son's bed expectantly. "What's going on, Jordo?"

"Dad, hey! It's one minute after midnight and I was told Saturday that I could tell you something Monday and you would believe me. It's technically Monday so I want to tell you, but I don't want you to think I have lost my mind and check me into a psych ward or anything."

Michael sat on the bed next to Jordan, "You can tell me anything, you know that. I won't think you're crazy."

"Yeah, well, I guess we'll see about that." Jordan paused briefly, but summoned the courage to push on. "At my party, I saw Christopher jump onto a rock wall and run down it. I told him not to because it was a steep drop off one side, but he didn't listen."

"No surprise there," Michael interjected.

"Yeah, well, he should have listened because he tripped and almost fell off," Jordan said.

"I didn't hear him say anything about that," Michael said.

"That's because it was a non-event for him. He tripped, but he regained his balance so quickly that he forgot about it when Amy came over. I think he likes her."

"Good grief," Michael sighed.

"Right! But that's not the important part. I don't think Christopher has any idea . . ." Jordan paused and took a deep breath before continuing. "But he didn't fall off of that wall because two angels flew in and saved him. One was on each side of him. They helped him regain his balance, and then they disappeared. Well, one did. The other told me to keep quiet about it and later told me that if I waited until today to tell you, that you would believe me. Mom is the one who believes in God and angels and all that, but this one told me specifically to tell you—not her."

Jordan sighed and sunk back in the bed, relieved to finally get it out.

Michael was stunned. "I actually do believe you, but I may not have yesterday. Do you remember what the angels looked like?"

"Not really. It's a little strange because they changed. I only saw one from the back, and he looked like he had on some kind of uniform, but he disappeared before I could get a good look at it. The other one was facing me. He looked tall, but it was hard to tell because he wasn't standing. He looked a little dirty, with something on his head, but when he put his finger to his lips to tell me to be quiet about what I was seeing, his outfit changed into a bright white robe and he flew away.

"Then, later when we started to open presents, one of them spoke to me, but I couldn't see him that time. It sorta freaked me out and made me calm down at the same time. He knew my name and read my mind, which was crazy, but then he said they were only there to make my birthday good. He said that if I waited to tell you that you would believe me. Do you?"

Michael just sat on his son's bed staring at the wall for a long moment. Finally, he said, "The reason I'm up is because I just had a dream, and I was trying to work it out in my head when I saw your light on. I think I may have met your angels when I was on my trip." Michael paused and thought about whether it was wise to continue. The truth was that he was relieved to have someone to talk to about it, so he took a deep breath and said, "They saved me from a couple of rough guys when I was there."

"You never said anything about that," Jordan said, trying to figure out if that news upset him or comforted him.

"I didn't want you to worry. Besides, it was really no big deal at the time. A couple of guys with guns wanted to kill me." Michael had to pause when he saw his son's reaction to those words. He put his finger up and continued. "But two men, a bedouin and an Egyptian police officer, came in and changed their minds." It seems those two men showed up again as angels at your party because you described exactly how they were dressed when I met them in Egypt. And they appeared to me again as angels in the dream I just had! Not only that, you say one of the angels knows my name and what I'm thinking." He tried to lighten the mood a little by adding, "Seems pretty clear we have a couple of angelic stalkers."

Jordan didn't laugh at his joke. Michael realized his son was still trying to process what happened to him in Egypt. "Why wouldn't you tell me that a couple of angels saved you from terrorists in the Middle East? That is so cool!" Jordan squealed.

Michael lowered his hand to remind the boy that there were sleeping girls in the house and to keep it quiet. "I didn't realize that there was anything unusual about those two men until the dream I just had, and I would never have considered that the dream was real until you said that you saw them too," Michael explained, putting it together for himself at the same time he was laying it out for his son.

"Does anyone else know about what happened to you over there?" Jordan asked.

"Only Adam and . . ." Michael stopped short and stared off into the distance, lost in thought about the conversation that his new friends had with him when fleeing the terrorists. Eve's calm prayer and Adam's insistence that God was protecting them flooded his mind. It wasn't until that moment that Michael actually thought long and hard about the familiar, yet unusual, names of the two people who had followed him home from Egypt.

"Dad?" Jordan prompted. "Dad, what is it?"

"Nothing. Nothing. It's just a crazy thought. Is there anything I can get you, punkin? I'm going to get some water and maybe a cookie."

"Sounds great to me too, but I'd rather have milk if I get to have a cookie. Gotta dunk it, you know?"

In the morning, Michael was on Jordan-duty, as Elise liked to call it. The dedicated father got up a little earlier than usual and went into the teen's room. He stood watching his beautiful boy sleep for a few moments before he decided to interrupt the peacefulness by hitting the off button on the BiPAP machine so he could remove his son's face mask. When the groggy boy smiled and raised his arms enough to free himself from the covers, Michael lifted him from the bed and placed him in the chair. After completing bathroom duties and dressing, they went to the kitchen for some breakfast. "What are ya having today, son?" Michael asked.

While they were enjoying their French toast, Jordan started describing a dream that he remembered. "I don't know what's going on with my head right now, but I guess it's because of all the angel talk before I went to sleep. This other dream was so weird though, Dad. You know how things you see and hear during the day can work their way into your dreams at night? The couple that stayed here all weekend was in my dream. I remember thinking yesterday in church when they were sitting beside us that it was funny to be there with a couple named Adam and Eve. I really didn't spend much time talking to them even though they were around for three days, but I guess their names stuck with me, and maybe that's why I dreamed about them. I mean seriously, how often do you meet a couple named Adam and Eve?"

"It *is* unusual and kind of funny, I agree. What happened in your dream?"

"I really don't remember much of it. All I know is that I was in this beautiful garden and I was running. I was actually running, Dad! Me! I had strong legs, and I was running fast too. It felt so good. I want to go back and run like that again. Anyway, I was running to get out, although I don't know why, and in front of me were your friends dressed in animal skins. Seriously, they looked like the real Adam and Eve. I asked them who they were, and they told me that I already knew and to trust that feeling. They said that you know who they really are too but haven't figured it out yet."

Michael just sat staring at his son pushing his French toast chunks into the puddle of syrup and laughing about what he was certain was a crazy, random dream. If the boy had tried, he probably could have knocked his father out of his chair with a halfhearted puff of breath, like a winded Big Bad Wolf. But Jordan didn't notice his father's reaction to what he was saying. Michael took a deep breath and willed himself to keep the crazy thoughts to himself until he was able to figure out what was going on. And he knew that something serious was going on with his family. It was at that moment that he became determined to find out what.

Michael got Jordan set up with a video game to play while he started on the rest of his morning routine. He looked at the clock and realized he was already running late, so he rushed through shoving the dishes into the dishwasher and started to head to the shower, but he couldn't make himself focus. No matter what he was doing, he couldn't shake the feeling that something more powerful than he had ever experienced before was pulling at him.

Even though time was running short, he crept to the bedside table in his room trying not to wake Elise on her morning to sleep in. He unplugged his cell phone and looked at it for a long time thinking he was being crazy, but he couldn't help himself.

"What are you doing?" Elise asked softly.

"Oh, I'm so sorry. I didn't want to wake you. I was just thinking about . . ." Michael sat on the edge of the bed and looked at his sleepy wife. "Elise, can I ask you a strange question without you getting all inquisitive about why I'm asking?"

"Uh, I guess," Elise responded, sitting up with a furrowed brow.

"Okay. Well if God wanted to tell somebody something, how do you think he would go about telling them?"

Elise's eyes grew big and she sat up straighter and smiled. "What do you think God is trying to tell you?" she squealed.

"Remember, no questions. Just answers."

"Oh, yeah. Right. Um, well, let's see. God speaks to people in many different ways. Some people say they can hear his voice. Sometimes we get nudges or ideas that he sends to us."

"Okay, but I mean like a message. Like he wants you to know something important."

Elise just pushed her eyebrows closer together and tilted her head at her husband. "In the Bible, God usually delivered special messages to people through dreams and visions. He still does that today, but you don't really hear about it much. Can you tell me what is on your mind? Please."

"Dreams and visions. Do you believe he still does that?"

"Absolutely. I think I'm having one right now," Elise said as she fluffed the pillow, collapsed back down into it and pulled the covers up to her chin. "If you decide you want to fill me in, I'll get up. Otherwise, I'm out."

"Of course. Sleep as long as you want. Jordan and I are fine. He's ready to go. I'll leave Amy's breakfast on the counter in case she emerges from her cocoon while I'm running Jordan to school."

There was no response from Elise. He kissed her lightly on the cheek and left the room, closing the door quietly behind him. Once he was alone, he decided to ask a question that could lose him the new friendship of a sane person, but he couldn't help himself. He typed a text message to Adam, "Hi. Crazy question for you and your lovely wife. Is it possible that you two are the REAL Adam and Eve?"

He sent the text then stared at his phone for a long moment before his heart raced at the small dot, dot, dot pulsing at the bottom of the text strand. When the words appeared, he stared at the tiny screen in disbelief: *It's not just possible. We'll stop by in a little while to talk to both you and Jordan, but only you two for right now, if that's okay with you.*

Chapter 16

Cole was sleeping on his arm when his teacher tapped the desk beside his head and said sarcastically, "So sorry to disturb your nap, but you have a note to go to the guidance counselor's office."

Cole sat up and collected his thoughts. He hadn't meant to doze off this time, really. It was the first time he had even made it to school since Lucy shattered his dreams after his drum solo, but it was time to pull himself together. He was frustrated with himself for not being able to even make it through one day of school without checking out, but he grabbed his book bag and the note and headed off to his appointment. When he got there, the counselor was busy moving papers around on her desk and scowling at the computer screen facing her. When she noticed Cole in her doorway, she put the papers down, took her glasses off and smiled. "Come on in, Cole. It is so good to see you. How have you been?"

Cole returned the smile, but couldn't help going on the defensive internally. *Office people are never really glad to see you*, he thought. *It's just more work for them. I wonder what is really going on here.* "I've been fine. How about you, Mrs. Thomas?"

"Can't complain. Well, at least it wouldn't do any good, now, would it?" The older woman giggled at her own wit and motioned for Cole to sit. She stared at her intertwined fingers for a moment before starting to explain the reason he was summoned to her office. "Cole, I don't know exactly how to put this, so I'm just going to tell you what I know, and then I am going to ask you to fill in the blanks. Can you do that?"

"Uh, sure, I guess," Cole responded. "What did I do this time?"

"That's just the thing. We're not really sure. The principal has asked me to see if we can figure out some things, and then he wants to talk to you."

"Mr. Parker wants to talk to me?"

"Maybe. We'll see," the counselor replied. "He came into my office yesterday morning and said that he was worried about you. He said that he shopped on Sunday at the grocery store where you work and didn't see you in there. He had to go back Monday after school and pick up an order for his wife and again didn't see you. He knows you work part time and that he probably just missed you, but the manager walked by when he was thinking about you, so he asked. You know that your manager Kevin is his son-in-law, right?"

"Yeah, I've seen them talking before and one time I asked Kevin how he knew him. Look, I know Kevin fired me yesterday for skipping work. He called and left a message for me to bring in my uniform and keys and that I no longer work there, but what does that have to do with school?"

"Well, as I said, I am going to start from the beginning and see if we can piece this thing together. Kevin told Mr. Parker that you missed your shifts on Saturday, Sunday, and again Monday after school and that you never called in, but that isn't why he fired you. He says you're a good worker and a good kid, but when he went to your house yesterday, he had no choice. He couldn't look the other way after what he saw. He would have been justified in letting you go just for missing your shifts without calling in, but he fired you because when he glanced through the back window of your car, he saw a case of beer that you had to have gotten from his store. The store's logo sticker was on the box, and when he checked with Kevin later, he was told that a case had gone missing on Sunday. The missing beer was the same brand that was in your car. Not only that, he said the front passenger side seat was littered with empty cans and your car was dented on the passenger side behind the wheel."

"So why am I talking to you? It seems like the cops should be here."

"As I said, there are some holes in what we know, and we are trying to piece things together. Hopefully, we won't have to call in the authorities, but it does look like you were drinking heavily, and we can't overlook that because of your age, especially if you drove the car while under the influence of alcohol. But that's where we get confused. Mr. Parker thought talking to me would help you to give us the answers we need before deciding what to do."

Cole was becoming more and more defensive by the minute. "What answers? It seems like you guys have all the answers. You think I stole a case of beer and got so drunk I dented in my car and decided to skip work and school. Where's the question?"

"Well, we can't make the timeline work, and we think there might be someone else involved. If it wasn't you who was drinking, then that just leaves you with the possession of the stolen beer, since it was in your car."

"Are you accusing me of stealing beer or not?" Cole snapped.

"Listen Cole, I am not trying to attack you. We are just trying to figure out what happened."

"Who exactly is 'we,' Mrs. Thomas?"

"Just Mr. Parker, Kevin the store manager, me, and your mother at the moment."

"My mother? What does she have to do with anything?"

"Mr. Parker called her a couple of hours ago and told her what Kevin found in your car and what the repercussions were as far as your job goes. He asked if she knew anything that would help us piece things together, but she couldn't shed much light on what you've been up to. She sounded frustrated that she hadn't been able to get you to leave the house. As far as she knows, you had been home sleeping or playing video games all day while she was busy working. So, Cole, can you tell me what happened last weekend?"

Cole sat expressionless in his chair, without indicating in any way that he was willing to tell his side of any story this guidance counselor may evoke. She waited for several moments before trying again. "Cole, you can answer my questions here if you want, but if you would rather I send you over to the police station to get the story, I will be glad to do that. Heaven knows I have enough to do without this."

Cole started to relax when he realized the counselor was grasping at straws. Maybe he could figure a way to avoid serious trouble. He took a breath and sat up straighter, willing himself to think objectively. "No, I'm sorry, Mrs. Thomas. I will answer the question. What was it again?"

"Who was with you?" the guidance counselor asked.

"When?"

The woman glanced at the notes on her legal pad. "I guess we need to go back to Friday night."

Cole answered truthfully. "I went to a party at our church. I'm a drummer in the band and was there all night."

Mrs. Thomas jotted something down and raised her pen for the next piece of the puzzle. "What time did you leave?"

"It was after midnight when we finally got out of there. We had to load all of the equipment into my friend's truck, and then we left."

The pen was poised and ready for the next move. "Where did you go then?"

Cole thought about telling Mrs. Thomas about his heartbreak and why he was upset, but what good would it do? That was personal, and he was determined to protect that secret. But he had gone to the grocery store when he left the church. He remembered going to the back where they keep the beer and had taken a case through the employee entrance to his car. He planned to pay for it later, but at the time he didn't know how else to get it. He was underage, so he couldn't buy it legally, and none of his older friends were there that night to cover the purchase for him, so he took it. Nobody would notice it was gone for a day or two, and by then he would have found time while he was working to ring in the sale himself and pay for it. If only he had remembered to go back and deal with that.

Maybe Mrs. Thomas had given him a solution, though. This mystery person could have bought the beer and the missing case would just be a coincidence. It seemed like the easiest cover story he could come up with on the spot, so he went with it. "Well, I am a little embarrassed, Mrs. Thomas, if you want to know the truth. I was a little stressed out that night, and I met up with a friend of mine after I left the church."

"What's your friend's name?"

Good question, Cole thought. "Sorry, but I'm not going to tell you that. I will tell you that he is older than twenty-one."

"Noted. Continue."

"Anyway, he was upset about a fight he'd had with his girlfriend and wanted to get some beer, so we drove to the store where I work to get some. He went in and bought it. I didn't go in with him, so I didn't see him pay, but I can't imagine he didn't. That's just not like him. Can you check to see if anyone paid for a case around midnight?"

"Yes, they already did, which is one of the reasons we are confused by all this. There were three cases of this type of beer sold between midnight and twelve thirty. Any of them could have been what was found in your car. Do you know if he had a receipt?"

"I really didn't ask," Cole chuckled inside. *This woman is messing up any chance the police will have to nail me,* he thought. *She should watch more TV.*

"That's okay. What happened then," the counselor prodded.

Cole thought hard. *I remember ripping the box open and pulling out the first beer, but then I noticed the security camera pointed in my direction. Last week the thing wasn't working, but I didn't know if it had been fixed and I didn't want to chance it. I decided to get out of sight, so I moved the car to a dark corner of the parking lot and backed into a space by the dumpster. There's no harm in saying that, I don't guess.* "Uh, yeah, my friend suggested we get out of sight, so we parked over by the dumpster. I think I hit the post when I tried to back in. I didn't have my lights on, and the lot isn't lighted over there."

"Right, so far that's what we thought. What happened then?"

This is where Cole had been getting stumped every time he tried to piece things together on his own. He honestly couldn't remember. All he could see when he tried to reconstruct the hours he spent sitting in his car by the dumpster drinking beer was a tall man in a red and blue plaid shirt and a baseball cap who approached his car from the driver side. He couldn't tell if the man was real or imagined, and he couldn't even remember whether he spoke to the guy or not. All he could remember was seeing the man approach the car, and the next thing he knew he was waking up in his bed at home. He didn't want to tell Mrs. Thomas, who apparently had the police on speed dial, that he was an underage blacked-out drunk beer thief, so he concocted the most believable story that he could.

"Ok, Mrs. Thomas, I'll tell you the whole story." She smiled and leaned in to listen more intently. Cole noticed she was holding that pen a little more tightly and had a new, clean page on the legal pad ready.

"Well, my friend was the one who wanted to drink. It was his beer, but I had been having a pretty rough night myself. So I decided to join him for a little while. I told him I just wanted a couple of beers, and I needed to go home, or it would be tough to get up and go to work the next day. So, he stashed the box in the back seat of my car, and we decided to go over by the dumpsters. I backed in and hit the post. My friend pulled in straight beside me, facing in the opposite direction so that we could talk easily—driver door to driver door. I passed beers through the window to him and when we were done with them, we tossed them into my passenger seat. He didn't want any evidence of drinking in his car because that's why his girl was mad at him. Remember, I told you he was upset about fighting with her?"

"Of course. Go on."

Cole was even believing the story himself. "Well, I sat there with him for a while and had a couple while he finished off most of the case. The more he drank, the more irritated he got. Eventually I was ready to leave, so I did."

"Your friend was obviously drunk, and you just left him to drive himself home?" the counselor asked incredulously.

Cole hadn't considered that. "Look, Mrs. Thomas, I'm no Boy Scout. And he's way older than me anyway. What was I supposed to do? Yeah, I left him. Maybe it's not smart or responsible, but there's also no law against leaving a store in your own car."

"Calm down, Cole. I'm just trying to put this together. But in the future, you should think about the well-being of your friends."

"He would have just said he was fine to drive, Mrs. Thomas. I really didn't even consider the fact that he wasn't. He drinks a lot. All the time, really. It's just the way he is, and he probably would have gotten mad at me if I acted like he couldn't handle a few beers."

"So, you drove home in your own car, by yourself," the counselor affirmed while she made a note on her legal pad.

I have no idea! Cole thought. "Yeah. I honestly only had one or two beers. I was fine," Cole stated.

"Do you know when that was?" she asked.

Not even a hint of a clue, Cole thought. "Not really. I didn't notice," he stated for her notes.

"Okay, so let's say all that is true. I still don't understand why you haven't come out of your house to go to work or school for so long. That's just not like you, Cole. Ditching school, maybe, but work, no."

"I told you I was having a bad night Friday. Can I just say it was about a girl and leave it at that?"

"Broken heart?"

"Something like that, I guess," Cole said, staring at his shoes.

"Sure. Thanks for talking to me, Cole. I'll let you know what we decide to do."

"Ok. Thank you, Mrs. Thomas," Cole said as he was leaving, and he meant it deeply. He knew she was the reason he wouldn't get into trouble. She had provided him with enough doubt of wrongdoing that nobody would take it further. He would have had no way of knowing they suspected another person was involved, or that three cases of beer were sold when he took his. All he had to admit to was drinking a beer or two, and now that he had done that, he could use it to his advantage. Not only was there a plausible explanation for almost everything, he didn't even need to go pay for that beer anymore. *Life is good*, he thought to himself, and for the first time in several days, he believed it.

Cole tossed his bag over his shoulder and looked at his watch. The bell for dismissal was only moments away, and he saw no need to return to class. He reached into his pocket for his keys and headed for the front door. On the way, he passed an acquaintance who had been at the church on Friday night. "Hey man!" the boy said. "I didn't know you could play like that. You rocked the place, man."

Cole paused briefly to offer a smile, thanks, and well wishes. He continued toward the doors but felt himself walking a little taller in response to the praise. He started to feel as if life after Lucy's rejection might be bearable after all. He pushed through the double doors at the entrance to the school and headed to the senior parking lot just as the dismissal bell sounded. There, by his car, was a tall man dressed in a red and blue plaid shirt and a baseball cap standing perfectly still with his arms crossed on his chest, staring right at him. Cole didn't change his heading, but he broke eye contact and looked away for a moment, searching his mind for a reason why this man looked so familiar. When the realization hit him, he looked back and yelled out, "Hey, I want to ask you something. . . ." But the man was gone.

Chapter 17

"What do you mean, they might be the *real* Adam and Eve? That's crazy, Dad!"

"As crazy as seeing angels save Chris from falling off a wall?" Michael shot back, putting his fingers to his lips to warn his son to keep things quiet.

Jordan shrugged and his face contorted with confusion. "They really said they want to talk to *me*? Why me? Do you think they know about me seeing the angels at the park?"

Michael smiled at his son, "I wouldn't be surprised if they know about your dream, to be honest."

"How could they know I had that dream if you didn't tell them?" Jordan asked with a stunned look on his face.

"I don't know, but there is something strange going on, and I hope they'll be able to explain it. I don't guess I need to twist your arm to get you to stay home from school today, do I?"

"Uh, no. You're not getting me to leave this house today, no matter what you and Mom do."

"Okay, but when they get here, don't ask them a bunch of questions. They said they just want to talk to the two of us, and your mom will be up soon. Just try and be patient and I promise, you'll get a chance to ask anything that you want. Deal?"

"Deal."

As if on cue, there was a soft knock on the door. He opened it and found Adam and Eve standing there smiling and holding a drink tray with six tall, delicious-smelling cups of coffee and a box of fresh doughnuts. "Good morning. How are you two doing?"

"Kinda freaking out, if you want to know the truth," Michael said as he reached appreciatively for the coffee Eve was handing to him and eyeing the box in Adam's hand.

"That happens. Can we come in for a bit and chat?" Adam asked gently.

Michael was genuinely happy to see his new friends, but the absurdity of his recent thoughts came to the front of his mind. "Absolutely, please come on in. But what do we say when Elise and Amy happen by and hear us talking? The things I want to ask you will be hard to explain away."

"Just let us worry about that," Eve said simply.

Michael didn't know what to say or to even think, so he turned his thoughts to what he could do in the moment. "Sounds great. Thanks for the coffee," he said reaching for the box of doughnuts. "And for these. They look delicious. Come in and make yourselves comfortable. I'll get some plates and napkins."

Jordan and Penny came into the room, both excited, but for very different reasons. Jordan eyed the goodies his dad placed on the table. Penny ran to Adam and jumped up, placing her front paws on Adam's thighs.

"Penny, get down!" Michael admonished. "Adam, I am so sorry. She never does that. She is a well-trained service dog. I've never seen her act like that before."

Penny obeyed the command, but could barely contain her excitement. She spun around and sat down, then stood and quaked all over. "It's alright, Michael," Adam responded as he squatted to pet the dog. "Animals love me for some reason."

He continued scratching her behind the ears. "Actually, I guess that's pretty much why we're here, isn't it? To discuss who we really are."

Michael laughed and wanted to reply, but before he could, Elise came around the corner in her favorite pink terry cloth robe, rubbing her eyes. When she noticed Jordan, she was jolted the rest of the way awake. "Jordan, why are you still here? Michael, why didn't you take him . . ." she stopped when she noticed Adam and Eve quietly sitting quietly at the breakfast nook cradling their warm coffee cups. "Oh, good morning! I look a mess!"

"You're beautiful," Eve said. "I hope you don't mind. We stopped by on our way out of town. We weren't planning on leaving the area for a couple of weeks, but the people we were staying with on Taneycomo had a family situation and had to go to Denver. We wanted to say bye to you and yours before we moved on."

"My goodness, I hope everything is alright with them and their family in Denver. Michael and I were commenting after you left church yesterday that we wished we could have spent more time with you guys just hanging out. You seem like such wonderful people, and the entire weekend we were rushing from one thing to another. If you aren't ready to leave Branson yet, feel free to bunk with us until you are."

"My, that is very generous of you," Eve said. "But we wouldn't dream of accepting until you four talk it over and agree that it's okay. We honestly have a bit of a gap in our schedule, and it would be lovely to stay a while longer."

Michael chimed in, "We'd love to have you." He looked at Adam with an expression that asked if the story Eve had told about their friends leaving town was true. By Adam's reaction, he could tell that it was, so he continued, "Please stay as long as you'd like." Jordan nodded his head in agreement.

Adam spoke up next. "To be honest Elise, it was Jordan that brought us by this morning. We have been praying for him and were craving an opportunity to spend some time talking with him and with his father. When we were in Egypt with Michael, he opened up to us about some spiritual matters, and some of them concern Jordan. So we would relish the opportunity to spend some time with them. If his not being at school today is a problem, we can certainly find another time to chat."

Before Elise could respond, the phone rang. Adam winked at Michael as if he knew something the rest didn't. When Elise answered the call and shrieked with joy, the others started to understand. The excited Elise asked her friend to hold on a minute and muted the phone while she explained to Michael that her friend and college-freshman daughter were in town for the day. She wanted to see if by any miracle Elise and Amy were free to spend it with them. Before waiting for Michael to respond, she unmuted the call and continued talking excitedly with her friend.

"Really, she is with you? How old is she now? Oh my goodness, I had no idea that she and Amy were that close in age. Yes, she is home on spring break." Elise glanced at the small group of onlookers in her kitchen and shrugged her shoulders. She held her hands palm up with a questioning look at her husband. Reading her expression, he nodded his head and gave a thumbs-up. She beamed and squealed to her friend, "You got it! I'm free. Nails, lunch, you name it."

Elise put the phone down and timidly rejoined the group. Her infectious smile prompted Eve to say, "I am so happy for you, Elise. It is such a rare treasure to reconnect with an old chum and to have such a welcome surprise when you and Amy are both available is a true gift."

Elise smiled warmly at her new friend, "It's unbelievable, if you want to know the truth. The last time we spoke was years ago, and I thought for so long that she was upset with me. It was so silly, really, but neither of us ever attempted to clear the air. I am so excited about the possibility of bringing her close again. And her daughter is almost Amy's age. I'm sure they will become fast friends. I am so excited to see them, but I wanted to spend the day with you guys. Are you sure it's okay for us to go?"

Michael answered, perhaps a little too quickly, but it went unnoticed by his wife. "Absolutely, sweetheart. Have a great time. Adam and Eve will be staying with us for a little while. I'm sure you and Amy will have plenty of time to spend with them later."

Elise clasped her hands in front of her chin and half-jumped. "Ooooh, I am so excited! What should I wear?" She didn't wait for a response as she spun around, sliding slightly on the hardwood floor in her sleepy socks and rushed off to wake Amy with news about their new plans. The four in the kitchen just sipped their coffee and smiled at the chain of supernaturally orchestrated events that they witnessed.

"Finally," Jordan exclaimed when the two women had left the house. "You two know angels?" he asked the biblical icons sitting at the table. "And you are the real Adam and Eve from the Garden of Eden?"

"Yes and yes," they answered in unison. Michael pulled up a seat at the table across from Adam, and Jordan maneuvered his chair into a spot next to Eve. "Yes, we know angels, but more importantly we know the One they serve. We are on a constant mission from God to travel the earth and try to make amends for the terrible sin that we committed in the garden."

"Yeah, about that," Michael said. "The Bible says you died as a result of eating the fruit." Adam smiled at Michael's recall of scripture. "Hey, I know some of it!" Michael added.

"Do you have a Bible handy?" Eve asked. When Michael returned with one, he slid it across the table to her. "Let's look at Genesis 1:29 together." She flipped through the first several pages of the book. "Michael, what does it say?"

Michael pulled it toward him and read the words to himself. He looked up and stated simply, "It says that you were given every seed-bearing plant throughout the earth and all of the fruit trees to eat for food."

"That's right," Adam said. "Now read to us what it says in chapter 2, verses 16 and 17."

Michael flipped the page and read out loud this time. "But the Lord warned him, 'You may freely eat the fruit of every tree in the garden—except the tree of knowledge of good and evil. If you eat its fruit, you are sure to die.' Yeah, everybody knows that. So what?"

"Yes, but what some people don't realize is that there were two unusual trees there and we were not forbidden from eating from any tree but the one. The other tree in the garden that was just as appealing and beautiful, incited our curiosity. It is known in the Bible as the Tree of Life. Earlier in the fateful day of our momentous mistake, we ate from that tree, but that event was not recorded," Adam stated.

Eve added, "Although not off limits, somehow we felt we were doing something wrong when we ate from that tree. It was the most delicious fruit we have ever eaten, but since nothing bad seemed to happen as a result of our eating it, we felt bold and powerful. Later, when we came across the serpent in the forbidden tree, he was easily able to convince us to give in to temptation and break the one rule that we had been given. I'm not trying to make excuses. What we did was wrong, even if we can see how it happened." Eve looked at her empty coffee cup and seemed to get lost in thought.

Adam continued. "God is a god of his word, and when he said that we would die as a result, we did in our own way. Personally, we were denied the right to pass on into eternity with our Lord as every other person born into this world has been gifted. Perhaps worse than that, we have to watch death claim every one of our descendants with the knowledge that their pain is our fault. It is heartbreaking at times."

"So, you will never physically die? Ever?" Jordan asked.

"Nope. But when Jesus comes back, he'll collect us with the other believers and will judge us on what we have done since our creation almost six thousand years ago. We honestly love people, because every single person on this planet is family. Unfortunately, we also carry a huge burden of guilt knowing that the harm that comes to each one is truly our fault. It is interesting to wonder what Satan would be doing if sin had not entered the equation. Since it did with us though, he has been having a party, and we were the ones who allowed that to happen."

"I thought I had problems!" Jordan said.

"You do. So sorry about that, son," Adam said smiling sympathetically.

Jordan just shook his head and continued his line of reasoning. "But it seems like I remember reading that you actually did physically die."

"Good memory! Genesis 5:5 tells the world that I was 930 years old when I died. It doesn't say how old Eve was, but I can tell you that as far as the world was concerned, she left it the same day I did."

"I spend a lot of time thinking about what will happen to my family after I am gone," Jordan admitted wistfully. "How did that all work for you two?"

"I'm so sorry that you carry that burden. It wasn't easy for us either. We had to walk out on those closest to us without saying any goodbyes or giving any explanations. You can choose not to suffer that way. Take the opportunity to say or to at least write what you feel toward loved ones when you feel it. Those words will be a continual gift to those you leave behind."

Michael looked at his son and wished with all of his might that the boy heard that advice and would remember it. He didn't say anything, though, and Adam continued. "To answer your question about how it worked for us, our bodies were growing old and frail, wrinkled and painful, but God would not allow us to leave this fallen world and experience his glory because of our sin. He was true to his word that we would be punished until he returns, but he needed to get us away from our immediate family in order for that to happen," Adam explained.

"Sometime around our nine hundredth year, two servants entered our lives. Caleb and Andel watched over our personal needs and were always at our side. Our family and friends became accustomed to their presence and trusted them with whatever need arose. One day we decided to take an overnight trip to a nearby town, and Caleb and Andel insisted that they would be the only ones to travel with us. Normally, we would travel with a large group, but they assured us and our family members that it wasn't too far for them to provide us with all the help and safety we would need. Once we got far enough away from home to be unnoticed, these two men revealed their true identities to us.

"Michael, you met them in Egypt, and Jordan, I believe you met them briefly at your birthday party."

"They were angels!" Michael exclaimed.

"They were and they still are. And they are here now. Would you like to officially meet them?"

Michael and Jordan just stared at each other's wide-open eyes before nodding in the affirmative. "Uh huh!" the boy sang out.

"Don't be afraid. They are friendly and wonderful," Eve said.

The island behind the kitchen table suddenly became the center of attention. On the other side, a human outline began to materialize in front of them. In mere moments, a man about six feet tall wearing a red baseball cap and a blue and red button-down plaid shirt stood with his hands placed on the island in front of him. "Nice to officially meet you two. I'm Caleb, Adam's helper."

Penny started to growl, but Adam's hand on her head calmed her, and she returned to her spot at his feet. Michael swallowed hard and willed himself to be calm. When he was able, he asked meekly, "Are you the police officer or the bedouin?"

"The policeman," Caleb chuckled.

"Thanks for that," Michael said seriously.

"No sweat, brother." Caleb turned to look beside him while another form materialized in front of them. Penny watched intently, but didn't growl this time. Instead, she just inched closer to Adam.

This man had curly brown hair and wore jeans and a plain green T-shirt. He smacked the granite countertop and winked at Eve. "And I am Andel. I serve God and Eve."

"The bedouin?"

"Yes, sir. At your service."

"Glad you don't just help Eve. Thanks for being there for me. It could have gotten bad."

"I'm afraid it would have. You are very welcome."

Jordan didn't respond, and Michael completely understood the mind-blank that he thought his son was experiencing. He had stood up from his chair when Caleb appeared and had placed his hand on Jordan's shoulder for moral support through what would be a monumental event for anyone, but especially for one with a weak heart. He rubbed his son's back absentmindedly when Andel joined them.

Eve smiled warmly at the display of affection between father and son. "You know, Jordan, your father has the same name as an angel. The name Michael means 'who is like God.' The archangel Michael is a mighty warrior who battles Satan and his angels."

"I didn't know that," Michael admitted. "That's pretty cool."

"It is. Anyway," Adam continued undeterred, "For us to continue living as people, our family needed to think we had died. Once we were away from them, these two, masquerading as our well-known and trusted servants, went to our family and informed them that we would not be returning from our journey."

"We didn't say they died," Andel offered. "But there was an uncharacteristic misleading that is not often asked of angels. We simply had to deliver a message that needed to be known."

"Once we were on our own, we had to start a new life," Eve continued. "We found a nice cool cave and moved in. During that time, our bodies started to change in the way that everyone who has ever lived wishes it would. Our skin grew tighter and our muscles regained strength and firmness. Our hair color returned and things stopped hurting."

"Was it like one of those glorified bodies I have heard about?" Jordan found the strength to ask.

"No, I don't think so," Adam answered. "Of course, we haven't had the opportunity to witness that yet, but we do know that when Jesus appeared to people after his resurrection, he was able to be touched and to eat. But he was also able to appear and disappear and to keep people from recognizing him. Our bodies behave normally."

"Not exactly normal," Michael mused. "I can't imagine what a scientist who dreams of immortality would do to you two. He would lock you up and take blood samples and clone, clone, clone!"

"That's one reason we are so careful about revealing ourselves," Eve commented. "We never know what's in a person's heart or mind, so we wait for the green light from our Father. If he says it is okay to tell you, we do. If not, we don't. Simple rule to live by."

"Can I tell Elise, though? She won't say anything. I promise," Michael pleaded.

"You may tell anyone anything you like, Michael. We would prefer that you wait until we're gone to explain things to her, but we won't ask you to do anything you don't want to do. We have been in scrapes before, but usually when our identity gets out, nobody really believes the person who is spouting the truth anyway. We just have to smile until it blows over."

"Can you tell me how long I will live?" Jordan said meekly, looking up sheepishly at Eve.

"No, baby, we cannot. All we can tell you is that as sorry as we are that you have to face death because of us, we can also honestly say that we are immensely jealous of you. We would love nothing more than to go to heaven and see our Lord and our family and to leave the troubles of this chaotic world behind," Eve answered.

"I guess."

"Let me ask you something, Jordan. How do you feel about your situation, when you allow yourself to think about it?" Adam asked.

"I don't see my disability as fatal. Life is fatal. Everybody dies, and it's up to God when that happens. Somebody driving in a car or crossing the street can die. Just because I have DMD, it doesn't mean that I am any more at risk than anyone else. Sure, I am going to die before I get old, but it can happen to anyone. I won't act like I'm a victim."

"That's a very mature attitude," Adam said.

Jordan shrugged his shoulders. "That doesn't mean that I don't get jealous from time to time. I would love to be a star on the football team and to run downfield and leap into the air to catch the winning pass. I dream of that. So sometimes I get super mad at the disease, but then I just realize that everybody has something in their life to deal with, and I go on."

Eve beamed. "You've learned how to suffer."

"What?"

She leaned in and patted his knee. "Every person that God wants to draw close to him is taught to suffer. We all have challenges presented that are unique to us as individuals, and it's our job to learn to suffer well. It's easy to be happy with God and sing his praises when everything is going the way you want it to. But it's another thing to have faith and love and appreciation toward your Creator when you're suffering."

"Yippee," Jordan said sarcastically. "I don't know any different, since I've been this way for as long as I can remember."

"No, Jordan, that's not what I mean. You have had a physical limitation for as long as you can remember. What's noteworthy is how you have learned to deal with a deeper pain every time you watch a football player leap into the air and grab the winning touchdown. You have accepted what you have been given, and you have learned to praise and love your Savior in spite of the daily challenges you face."

Michael could tell that his son had no idea what to say. He smiled as the boy skillfully changed the subject. "Hey, did Dad tell you I'm a mutant?"

Eve's brow furrowed. "A mutant?"

"Yeah. About seventy percent of DMD cases are genetic, but the other thirty percent are spontaneous mutations. That's what I have, so I'm am a real-life mutant!"

"Professor Charles Xavier would be honored to have you join his team," Michael said.

"You know it!" Jordan sat up as tall as he could in his chair, surveyed his listeners and declared, "So guys and great-great-grandma, I don't have to go to school today, and I have two angels, two biblical heroes, and my awesome dad to entertain me. What are we going to do with this day that the Lord has made? I sort of feel like anything is possible."

Chapter 18

Christopher erased the Snapchat message for the third time before gritting his teeth and sending it. Besides, he was just asking Amy to go get a milkshake with him. It was no big deal. So why did it seem like an eternity passed before he received the reply?

"Sure, Chris, that sounds great. Do you want me to ask Jordan to join us? And do you want to meet us there?"

Great! Chris thought sarcastically. *How do I get out of that one?* Chris typed, erased, typed, erased, and was relieved to get another message from Amy before sending his response.

"Jordan can't go with us. Mom says he needs to rest. Do you still want to go, or should we postpone?"

Chris's head was spinning. "No, that's ok. I'll pick you up in about an hour if that's alright with you. Jordan can join us next time." He sent the message and briefly considered shutting his phone down to keep from getting a response that would change the plan. Instead, he paced back and forth in his room, staring at the tiny screen and waiting for the green light. He desperately wanted to pick Amy up in an hour for their first date, even though she had no idea that he was even interested in her in that way.

"Ok, see you then," appeared on his screen, and he felt as if he could fly. He immediately started digging through the laundered shirts in a basket on his bed before sifting through the ones hanging in his closet. Ultimately, he chose a shirt that he forgot he even had and changed into his favorite jeans.

Precisely one hour later, Chris pulled into her driveway. He turned the motor off, glanced at his hair in the rearview mirror and started to get out of the Jeep. He had just opened his door and set his left foot on the pavement when she came out of the house. She was dressed in an oversized sweatshirt, ratty jeans, and sneakers. Her hair had been hastily pulled up into a doubled-over ponytail, and she had her school book bag thrown over her shoulder. His heart sank for a moment until he realized it didn't matter. After all, she had no idea that he wanted this to be a date. All she knew was that she was going to get a milkshake, and she agreed to go even though it was clear that it would only be the two of them. *That's fine,* he told himself. *It's just us. That's all that matters.* His smile returned and he greeted her warmly as she climbed into the passenger seat.

"I hope you don't mind," Amy said as she hooked the seatbelt and dragged the book bag's zipper to open it. She pulled out a textbook on teaching elementary school language arts to show him the cover. "I have a project that I need to work on, and I thought with your creative mind and artistic eye, you could help me with it while we try all the new flavors of milkshakes they have out this season."

"Sounds fun," Chris said. "I'd be glad to help." *At least we have something to talk about!* he thought.

They chose a cozy corner booth in the 1950s-themed restaurant, and Amy pulled out the textbook again. Chris reached across and spun the book around so that he could see it better and started to flip through the pages while she explained the assignment.

"We have to come up with a unique way to teach upper elementary school kids how to write. It's tougher than you might think. I mean, you just write, you know? I'm not talking about teaching them how to form letters or even how to use commas or to explain the difference between words that sound alike. It needs to be about actually writing a story or something like that."

Christopher was listening intently and trying his best to help. "Like, what type of writing? Does it matter?"

"What do you mean?"

"You said it needs to be a story. Can it include conversation, or is it supposed to be descriptive or poetic?"

"See? I knew you could help. I don't really think there are any restrictions about what they write, as long as it gets them writing."

Christopher sat there thinking for a moment while Amy started picking at the plate of chili cheese fries that the singing waitress just placed between them. "Well, I have two ideas," he began. "It would be better if I could show you what I am thinking instead of trying to explain it. You up for that?"

"Sure! I've been racking my brain on this for two days, and I've got nothing. If you have an idea, I would love to see it."

Chris tried to hide his grin as he stood up from his booth seat and came over to her side. "Do you mind scooting over? It'll be easier this way."

Amy rearranged the dish of fries and their shakes so that Chris could settle in. He pointed to her bag and asked for paper and something to write with. Once he had what he needed, he started doing what he does best. He started to draw.

Amy watched his pencil work and was mesmerized by the scene that developed as she watched. "Wow, you're good. Is that supposed to be me?"

Christopher hoped it wasn't obvious how much time he had spent recently learning to draw a cartoon version of her. He hoped it looked spontaneous and skillful, and from her reaction, he thought it did. "Yeah. That's you, and this over here is going to be me. My idea is to start the lesson by getting the kids to draw. It doesn't have to be elaborate or even any good, but you should challenge them to create a character they like. It might take a couple of tries, but keep at it. Once they have a character they are excited about, you can create as many writing prompts and lesson activities as you could possibly need. Starting out, you tell them to think about their unique character, and then you can give them a prompt and instruct them to draw their unique character in the situation the prompt dictates. It can be anything, like washing the car or playing kickball on the playground or going bowling or whatever you want. The first challenge you present to them is to draw a comic strip showing their character in the scenario."

The whole time Christopher was talking, he continued to draw. Before long he had three cartoon boxes next to each other. The first one showed cartoon versions of him and Amy sitting on opposite sides of the table drinking milkshakes. In the second panel, the two characters were on the same side of the booth, and Chris's character was drawing in a notebook. In the third panel, three little kids held up papers each with a large letter *A*.

Amy was impressed with the speed and quality of the artwork, but Chris didn't respond to the compliments. Instead, he tried to explain his vision. "Okay, so that's the first step. Get the kids to tell a story using simple pictures in cartoon boxes. After they fill in the speech bubbles above the characters' heads, you are set for my second idea—teaching them to write dialogue."

"What do you mean?" Amy asked, intrigued by his idea.

"Well, you said you have to teach them something about writing. So you can show them that whatever appears in the speech bubble is what goes in quotation marks, and you can explain that what is in the bubble is set off with a comma. If they are describing the scene, which does not include anything spoken, with no bubbles, then it doesn't use quotes. What do you think?"

"Man, Chris, that's brilliant! How did you come up with that so fast? I have been trying to figure out something since I heard about the assignment, and I got nowhere."

"Well, I guess I'm always thinking about scenarios in cartoon form. It just seemed like an idea I could help you with."

"Yeah, I guess. I mean you were in calculus class trying to make the perfect face for a happy and sad letter X. You're definitely focused on what you want to do with your life, I'll give you that."

"I guess. These any good?" Chris asked reaching for a fry.

"They were great. They're getting a little cold now though. I guess you were distracted by my homework, huh?"

"I don't mind. I enjoy stuff like this."

It was great to spend this alone time with Amy, but it felt even better to help her by doing something he enjoyed so much. He loved cartooning and was reminded again how much he wanted to devote his life to that line of work.

Chapter 19

"Elise, you don't need to apologize at all. Adam and I relish every minute that we can spend with Jordan, but we're elated that he has this opportunity. I know it's important for him to spend time with friends at a place where he can truly be himself. We'll have a chance to chat with him on the way there and on the way back, and your idea of taking in a show on Saturday sounds great. We couldn't have planned a more perfect weekend if we tried."

Elise's head was buried in the refrigerator, looking for something to offer her guests. "That's so understanding of you," she said, closing the fridge door and putting her hands on her hips. She glanced around and saw a wrapped-up plate of cookies by the sink. She reached for them and continued. "Jordan loves these kids and looks forward to the weekend at the lake every year. Normally, our life is so mundane, but not lately. It seems like ever since you arrived, we've had an abundance of things to do. I am so sorry."

"Don't worry about entertaining us, Elise," Eve said again, waving off the offer from her host to have a cookie. "We're fine and enjoying every minute that God has given us to spend together."

Jordan rolled in as Eve finished speaking. "Sup homies? What's going on in here with the old folks?"

"Jordan!" Elise barked at her son. "That's not polite."

Eve winked at Adam, and they shared an *if Elise only knew how old Jordan means* look and smiled at each other. Penny approached Adam, gave him a lick on the hand, and settled in under the table, leaning against his legs.

"Yeah, well, whatchya talkin' about anyway?" Jordan said without a hint of remorse over his perceived rudeness while reaching for the plate full of cookies.

"About your exciting weekend coming up. Tell us about it," Adam encouraged.

"It's awesome! My friend Sam has a place up at the lake and it's huge, and some kids that we know from PPMD come in from all over for this weekend together every spring."

"PPMD?" Adam questioned.

Elise knew Jordan could explain, but she took the reins anyway. "Parent Project Muscular Dystrophy is an amazing organization founded by a wonderful lady named Pat Furlong. It's the largest grassroots organization in the world that's focused on bringing the medical and political community together to find a cure for Duchenne muscular dystrophy."

"And they put on this event at the lake every year?" Eve asked, trying to organize her thoughts while pouring Jordan a glass of milk.

"No," Elise explained. "It's just put together and run by parents of kids that met through PPMD. The organization doesn't have anything to do with it, but it has become a weekend that we all look forward to every year. We call it a retreat weekend because Sam's parents provide such a wonderful environment close to all of the entertainment Branson has to offer."

Eve interjected, "So, it's like a mini-vacation for everyone. The kids have social time with others they don't get to see very often, and the parents have time to enjoy themselves without the guilt. That sounds like a terrific idea."

Elise nodded in agreement. "Yes, and Mr. Elliott is aware of the boys' special needs, so there's less worry for the parents in leaving their kids there. Every year he hires a pair of certified nurses who split the time and stay there with the kids all day and all night. But the parents do have to help. We take shifts running activities and dealing with meal preparations. When we aren't on duty, we generally escape to the madness of downtown Branson and enjoy some time without the constant worry of patient care. It's a nice break for everyone."

"It sounds wonderful. When is your shift to work?" Eve asked as she settled back into her seat at the counter.

"First thing, which is great. We'll be there when everything gets started and will be on duty until the kids go to bed Friday night. Then, we're free the entire day on Saturday and will go back about lunchtime on Sunday. Did you get a chance to look at the online description of the show *Samson* at the Sight and Sound Theater?"

"We did." Eve said, as Adam nodded in agreement. "It looks wonderful. I can't wait to see the stage. It said on the website that it envelops the audience, coming around on three sides, so you have a great view from every seat. It sounds like quite a production."

Jordan started driving his wheelchair forward about a foot and then reverse about a foot over and over until it got some attention. "Yes, dear. You have something you wish to say?" Elise prodded sarcastically.

"Uh, yeah. I haven't even gotten a chance to tell everyone my ideas for Minecraft this year."

"Minecraft?" Adam asked.

"Yeah. It's an online game where the player creates his own world, and then he lives in it. It's fun by yourself, but it's even better when you have a bunch of people working on it together. We have teams and build a new world together every year."

"Why is it called Minecraft?" Adam asked, trying to understand.

"Because in order to build things, you have to mine the materials. You use blocks of dirt, stone, ores, wood, water, and lava to build things."

"And there's the craft part, huh?" Adam guessed.

"Basically. Wanna hear my ideas?"

Before Adam could answer, Elise interrupted. "Wouldn't it be more fun to wait until the presentation on Sunday and explain things when you can actually show us what you and your friends built?"

"Fine. I guess," Jordan said somberly, but then he exclaimed. "And I'll be wearing the crown when I explain the good parts that I thought up. Okay, I'll wait."

Elise was relieved, knowing that she just saved her guests from an unending soliloquy on computer graphics that none of them would understand. She turned to her guests to explain. "When the kids finish creating their new world this weekend, they have an hour set aside to show it off to the adults. They take us on a virtual tour of everything, and when they're showing us something, the child who developed the particular component gets to wear the crown while he explains."

"A crown?" Eve asked with raised eyebrows.

"Yeah. Danny's mom made it with aluminum covered cardboard and plastic gems glued to it the first year, and we keep using it. There are better ones that you can buy from party stores, but the one we have has been with this group from the beginning, so it's special to us all. The MVB gets to keep it for the year and is responsible for crowning the next year's MVB."

Adam couldn't help himself. "MVB?"

Jordan beamed. "Most valuable builder—and this year it's going to be me. Danny got it last year because he figured out that he could build doorways with a block at the bottom to step over, and it kept the zombies out all night. It saved us a lot of building time inside the mansion since we didn't have to worry about them getting in."

At the mention of the word zombies Eve's face contorted. "Oh my," she said.

Michael had joined the group several minutes earlier and was enjoying a cup of coffee while listening to the conversation. It didn't take him long to be up to speed, and Elise noted that when Eve looked concerned, he was quick to jump into defense mode. "It's harmless fun, really. The figures look more like LEGO people than anything scary. They're just obstacles that present the players with problem-solving scenarios."

Eve apparently wasn't convinced. All she said in response was, "Hmmmmmm."

"How many kids come together for this party?" Adam asked.

Elise smiled and relaxed, happy once again to be on a safe topic. "It varies, but this year it looks like we'll have six come to the lake house, and with Sam that makes seven."

Adam smiled. "Tell me about the kids. Is it a mixture of boys and girls?"

Jordan was the one to answer first. "No. Girls can get DMD, but it's very rare. I don't personally know of any girls with it."

Elise picked up the answer to Adam's question from there, "All six of the kids coming in have Duchenne, but the host,

Sam, has a severe form of Becker muscular dystrophy. He's the only one not in a chair at this point. The kids coming in besides Jordan are from New Jersey, Louisiana, Virginia, Texas, and Romania."

Adam raised his eyebrows, "That's quite an accomplishment to get a group like that together every year."

Elise nodded her head while she finished chewing on a cookie, "Honestly, the location is what makes it such a success. All of the entertainment that a big city has to offer coupled with the serenity of the lake house makes it perfect for these families to enjoy themselves. We're so thankful that Sam's dad has continued to invite us all year after year."

Chapter 20

Cole sat in his desk at the back of the classroom, his head tilted back resting on the wall and his gaze fixed on the ceiling. His fingers tapped out a tune, silent to his closest neighbor but filling his mind with rhythm. His teacher was droning on about something, but he wasn't interested. His world was in chaos, and school wasn't going to help. His mother was angry about his drinking again and had taken away his car for anything other than driving to school. His efforts to win Lucy's heart had fallen short. Last night he had received a call from the lead singer of one of the church bands he played for. He tapped on the desk while mentally rehearsing the singer's words. "Cole, I'm sorry. It's not up to me. What Pastor Joe says goes. If he doesn't approve of us, he'll just use another band, and we can't afford that. There's nothing I can do, man. He said that your drinking isn't the type of message he wants to preach. I'm sorry, Cole, but at least for now, you're out."

"I don't have a drinking problem," Cole pleaded. "You know that. I was just upset that night and got caught. It won't happen again."

His friend explained that the word had also spread to the other groups he sometimes played for. The bottom line: Cole was a drummer without a band, a teenager without a car, and a young man without a girl.

Cole snapped to attention when the teacher appeared in front of his desk and slid a piece of paper under his tapping fingers. "You can do better than this, Cole," she said as she shook her head slightly and continued to the next row to pass out the remaining sheets. Cole focused on the paper, and then the bell rang. He tried to read it while hoisting his backpack from the floor and looping a single strap over his shoulder. His momentum halted when he realized what he was reading. He scanned the paper again and looked for any passing marks on his interim report. When he found none, he crumpled the paper into a tight ball and tossed it into the trash can on his way out the door.

Several people spoke to him as he walked through the halls to his next class, but he was unaware of them. His head started to pound, and the muscles in his jaw tightened as he thought about this latest setback. His mother would be furious if he didn't graduate. He hadn't found another job yet, and he knew that his mother needed him to work. She needed him to help with the bills, but she was willing to juggle that responsibility alone as long as he worked to make something of himself, which now seemed unlikely. How was he going to get all of his grades up in just four weeks? It was too much for him.

Instead of turning right to go to his next class, he turned left and blew through the doors leading to the senior parking lot. He threw his bag in the back seat, cranked the engine, and squealed his tires as he sped out of the parking lot.

Moments later, he pushed through a paint-chipped door with a Harley Davidson sticker in the window. He hadn't planned on going to a bar, but there he was—eyes widened to take in the details of the darkened room. He entered slowly and selected an out-of-the-way table to spend the afternoon.

The bar was smoky, but not as bad as he guessed it would be in a few hours. Only a handful of people were currently inside. The bartender appeared to be taking inventory but looked up and offered a friendly greeting to the potential paying customer.

On the far side of the room, a tall man, dressed in a blue and red plaid shirt and a baseball cap played darts alone. Cole recognized him instantly and decided to learn the man's identity. Before confronting the man, though, he went to the bar and ordered a beer, showing a fake ID that he suspected the bartender knew was fake but didn't care. He accepted the beer, took a refreshing drink from the bottle, and approached the stranger at the dartboard.

"Hey," Cole said awkwardly.

"Hey, yourself," the stranger replied, continuing to line up a dart and throw it.

"Want company?" Cole asked.

"Not really," the man replied.

Cole didn't know what to do or say, so he just pulled up a chair and sat silently watching the man practice. After the man returned from collecting his darts from the board to throw another round, he saw Cole watching him and silently returned to his place to try again. After a couple of darts, he turned to Cole and asked, "What can I do for you, son? Shouldn't you be in school or something?"

"I guess," Cole replied, working on his beer.

The man stood in front of the boy with a single dart in his right hand and the rest in his left. "You want something from me?"

"Not really. I just want to know if you have ever seen me before."

The man grunted and went back to his throwing.

"I just keep seeing you, is all," Cole said loudly enough for the man to hear him over the whir from the blender running on the other side of the bar.

The man looked at Cole briefly then finished throwing the remaining darts at the board. He sighed and seemed to resign himself to an odd conversation with a stranger. He stayed standing, but he let his arms drop and turned his attention toward the boy. "So, son, where is it that you think you saw me?" the man asked.

Cole thought about how it would sound to answer truthfully, but it didn't seem to matter. "Well, the first time, I was sitting in the parking lot at a grocery store drinking a beer."

"A beer?" the stranger said, raising his eyebrows.

"Okay, man, a case of beer. The second time, I saw you standing by my car in the school parking lot, looking right at me."

"Told ya you should be in school," the man snickered.

"Whatever, man. What's going on? Now, I come in here to blow off some steam, and here you are again. So, who are you?"

"So you were drinking the first time, in trouble at school the second time, and in a bar skipping school the third time. It seems to me as if you have enough to worry about without wondering who I am."

"I didn't say I was in trouble at school the second time."

"Weren't you?"

"Yeah, I guess I was. But how would you know that? And who are you?"

"Lucky guess. Name's Caleb." He stuck out his hand for Cole to shake it. "I guess I have a habit of showing up. Wrong place at the wrong time, or right place at the right time, or something like that, I guess. I promise you, son, I mean you no harm."

Cole looked into the eyes of a man throwing darts in an empty bar at lunchtime, which made him seem like an unemployed crusty old dude Cole had no interest in. But something about him pulled at Cole. "What's your story?" the boy asked.

The man grunted with a laugh and threw the remaining darts. He sat down with Cole, rested his elbows on the table, and clasped his hands together in front of him. "None of your business. That's my story. You seem like you're the one who wants to talk, son. Why don't you tell me *your* story?"

Cole knew the man was right. He didn't know why he wanted to talk, but he felt at ease around Caleb, and he desperately needed someone to listen. "Nothing's going on, really. I just got bummed 'cuz I'm failing out of school, and my mom is depending on me to graduate."

"Coming to a bar in the middle of the day isn't going to help you pass math class, son."

"I know. I think it may be too late," the boy confessed. "There's no way to get my average high enough in most of my classes to even make it."

"Is it imperative that you have a diploma? What are you going to do with it?"

"I don't know, man. You're supposed to get a diploma so you can get a decent job and all that," Cole stated weakly.

"I understand, but what type of job do you want? Do you need a diploma? Not all jobs require one. Seems to me that if you can't get the grades up high enough at this point to earn a diploma, you still have the option of getting a GED."

Cole hadn't allowed himself to think about taking that route, but he saw the logic in it. He changed the subject to his frustration over Lucy and the financial trouble that he and his mother faced without him working. He vented over being stupid enough to get fired from an easy job and about the difficulty in finding a new one.

He never even noticed that throughout the hour or so that he vented all of his problems to this stranger, he didn't feel the need to get a second beer. He would have been surprised, if he had checked, that he hadn't even emptied half of his first one.

"What should I do, Caleb?" he asked with exasperation.

"Let me ask you something, Cole. Do you know Jesus?"

"Jesus? Yeah, sure, I guess. I'm a drummer in a praise band, and I've been around church my whole life."

"That's great, Cole. But do you know Jesus?" Caleb asked again without taking his eyes off Cole's.

"Of course, I know who Jesus is. I just told you, I am around church all the time, and I play music about him all the time. He is the son of God and died for our sins."

"That's better, Cole. But I ask you again—do you *know* Jesus?"

"What do you want me to say, Caleb?"

"I want you to admit to yourself that you don't know Jesus."

"Why would you say that? You don't know me!" Cole snapped.

"I know that if you have this stack of problems to deal with and you know Jesus, you would dump it all at his feet. And you would not be in a bar talking to some random guy playing darts about some very real questions."

Cole just stared at Caleb and didn't know what to say. Caleb continued, "The good news is, Cole, that I do know Jesus, and I would be willing to help you through this if you like."

Cole pushed himself away from the table. He shook his head as he got up and started to head for the door, but by the time he got there, he changed his mind. He turned around to see that

Caleb had returned to the dartboard and had already thrown one into the bull's eye. "Alright, Caleb. I would appreciate your help. The truth is, I don't know who else to talk to."

Caleb smiled at the boy and said, "Okay, then. I know everything in your problems list. Now, tell me about what makes you happy. What do you enjoy, and what would you like to see yourself doing for the rest of your life? You talk. I'm throwing."

"You in a darts tournament soon or something?"

"No. Never done it before, if you want to know the truth. I like it!"

While Caleb continued throwing darts, Cole droned on about his devotion to Lucy, his involvement in church bands, and his passion for playing the drums. After a long time revealing his innermost thoughts, Cole felt both relieved and irritated. It felt good to get it all out without being judged, but he expected some wisdom from this dart-throwing man who claimed to know Jesus. But all Caleb said was that Cole should take what he learned in church for all those years and decide to trust Jesus, which meant that he needed to lay his burdens at Christ's feet. Caleb also looked Cole directly in the eyes and smiled as he said he would pray for him.

Cole left the bar disappointed, but Caleb was elated.

Chapter 21

Christopher sat at his desk staring at the three opened letters in front of him. The first one he expected, but it still made him mad. His application to attend the College of the Ozarks had been rejected, as he knew it would be. The free tuition made admission extremely competitive, and when your goal in life is to draw cartoon figures, sometimes things like studying for an AP chemistry test are overlooked. Looking at the letter made him think about Jennifer and the plans they had made. They both applied to C of O as a strategy to stay together and close to home. That plan bit the dust a while back, but this latest nail in the coffin of their dreams hurt anyway. He shoved it aside to concentrate on the real decision he had to make.

Two acceptance letters, one from the Savannah College of Art and Design—known as SCAD—and one from Ringling College of Art and Design, sat on the desk. Ringling was his dream school, but it was the more expensive choice. For tuition, room and board, books, and supplies, he was looking at close to sixty thousand dollars a year. SCAD was only about ten thousand less when all tallied up, but ten thousand dollars a year savings over the course of his education would be significant for his parents. He desperately wanted to want the cheaper option, but he didn't. Ringling had been his dream for almost a decade, and he didn't want to let it go—especially since he had the acceptance letter in his hand. He hadn't yet heard if he qualified for any grants or scholarships, so he held onto his optimism.

The longer Christopher sat and stared at the two letters, the more frustrated he became. He pushed himself away from the desk and thought that he should just enjoy the moment he had looked forward to for so long. He was accepted at his top two schools, and he would figure out what to do about specifics later. He pulled his phone out of his pocket and dialed Amy.

"Oh, Chris, that's wonderful," Amy said. When he explained the choice that he was facing, she said, "Oh, well that's a lot of money. I'm sure that wherever you do your little drawings, the teachers will see you have talent. You will get a good job from either one, I'm sure."

Christopher knew she was trying to be excited for him and supportive of the sentiments behind the decision, but she just didn't get it. He needed someone to tell him what he wanted to hear. Not only had she not done that for him, she called his life's work and dream for his future "little drawings." He was more upset after he hung up the phone than when he dialed it. Before he realized what he was doing, Jennifer said, "Hello?" from his phone.

"Hey, Jen. How are you?" Christopher asked softly.

"I'm great. How are you, Chris? I was thinking about you the other day. Have you heard from anyone yet?"

"Yeah. That's why I called, but first I wanted to know what you've heard."

Jen sighed loud enough for him to hear. "Well, you know I got in at Mizzou, and I was also accepted at Robert Morris, and I just got the acceptance to C of O yesterday." Christopher was irritated at the last tidbit of news. It shouldn't have stung, but it did. Jen always studied for her AP chemistry tests.

"Still going to Mizzou, though, right?"

"Yeah. I almost wish I didn't get in at the College of the Ozarks. That way, my parents wouldn't feel like I should take the free option. I just have my heart set on the bigger school further from town and having Candice as my roommate."

"I get that," Chris said. "I am facing that myself. I got in at both SCAD and Ringling, and the money thing is big."

"Chris, you're such a goof. You know you have to go to Ringling. If you don't, you'll regret it for the rest of your life. Your parents can swing it, and you know they'll do anything in the world for you. Just check the acceptance box, and ask your parents if you can send it in. I promise, they'll be as excited as you are."

"It's so much money, though, Jen. I feel really bad about it."

"You know you'll get help. The grants and scholarships will come through. I know that without a doubt in my mind. You have so much talent and you're so committed that your portfolio will come through for you. Just believe in yourself. It'll work out. I bet after you hear from everyone, Ringling will actually cost your parents less than SCAD would."

"I miss you, Jen. I needed to hear this. Thank you," Chris felt a lump in his throat, but he pushed it down.

"I miss you too, Chris. I am so glad you called. I was wondering how things were going with you."

Chris thought he heard hope in her voice. He had come this far, he had to try. "You wanna go get a burger tonight with me?"

"Oh, Chris, I don't think that would be a good idea."

His heart dropped. How did she still have such power over him? "Do you have plans?" he asked.

"Well, honestly, yes. But if I didn't, my answer would still be the same. I have started to heal, Chris. If we go out, it might send me back to where I was, and I can't go through that again. I'm so sorry. I need to get off the phone. Congratulations on getting into Ringling, Chris. Really. Bye."

Chris just stared at the screen that indicated the call had been terminated and he plopped down onto his bed. *That girl can send me through the clouds one minute and slam me back down the next*, he thought. *She's right though. I need to go to Ringling. May as well get this over with.* He grabbed his acceptance letter and went to find his mother.

Chapter 22

"He did what?" Cole's single mother, Sonya, shrieked into the phone. "When?" Sonya listened for a moment before sitting down to hear the rest. "No, I had no idea he was thinking about that. Thank you for calling, Mrs. Thomas. I'll talk to him and call you back at the beginning of the week."

What in the world am I going to do? Sonya thought to herself. *I just can't handle this anymore.* She took the top off of the bottle of extra-strength pain reliever and shook three tablets into her hand.

Admitting to herself that she was at the end of her rope shook Sonya to her core. How had her life taken such a downward turn? Her husband had died several years earlier from a long struggle with colon cancer. His hospital bills had depleted the money they had saved over the years, and the funeral expenses, even after the insurance company paid their part, left Sonya and Cole without much to live on. Cole was finally old enough to pitch in and help pay the bills, but losing his job recently had thrown her into turmoil. She tossed the three tablets into her mouth and washed them down with a glass of water.

Sonya sat on the edge of her seat in the kitchen, holding her head in her hands. Her elbows dug deeply into her thighs, but she didn't notice. The crisis of the moment was a choice between commitments—to work or to her son. Both needed Sonya's attention and were her highest priorities. Her son was spinning wildly out of control, and if he ever needed her to be there for him, it was now. But she had eagerly agreed to work all weekend, and there were a lot of people depending on her.

For the third year in a row, Sonya had happily agreed to be one of the two hired certified nurses for the annual DMD sleepover at the lake. It was good money, and she signed up without hesitation to split the work with her friend Shelby. Each had agreed to work two twelve-hour shifts, committing Sonya from eight p.m. until eight a.m. Now that it was time to go, however, her migraine made her doubt whether she was doing the right thing.

While she sat pondering the situation, Cole banged in through the door, jolting her out of her internal strife. "Hey, Ma!" he said cheerily.

"Cole, what's going on with you?" his mother asked bluntly.

"Nothing. Got anything to eat?" Cole said, burying his head in the refrigerator.

"Cole, seriously, could you sit with me a minute. I need to go soon," Sonya pleaded.

"You mean you didn't dress up in your all-white nurse get-up 'cuz you're bored?" Cole commented, pulling up a chair. "What's up, Ma?"

"I just got off of the phone with your guidance counselor," she stated.

"Again? Man, that woman just won't leave me alone," Cole whined. "What does she want now? To accuse me of stealing more beer?"

"No. I think they dropped all that," Sonya said. "They pulled the video footage of you leaving the parking lot that night at three in the morning. What on earth were you doing there until three in the morning?" Sonya asked and then reconsidered.

"Never mind. I don't want to know. But they saw the guy who was driving your car on the surveillance camera. They never saw his car in the parking lot, but they could see him on the camera as he drove your car out of the lot, I assume to bring you home. So you have proof that you didn't drive while under the influence."

Cole appeared thoroughly confused, but Sonya just thought it was an act, so she continued. "Anyway, she was calling about . . ."

Cole interrupted her, "Hold on, Ma. What did the guy look like?"

"What?"

"The guy who drove me home. Did they say what he looked like?" Cole still appeared confused, but this time Sonya didn't overlook it.

"Don't you know who was in your car with you, Cole? How would I know what he looked like?"

"Did they say anything at all?" Cole fished.

"I think they said he had on a baseball cap. That's all I know. Anyway, Cole, she was calling about your visit in there today. What are you thinking?" Sonya asked, pushing the button on her phone to check the time.

Sonya stared at her son, waiting for a response, but his mind seemed to be occupied elsewhere. "Cole!" she shouted, bringing his attention back to her. "What are you doing talking to the guidance counselor about getting a GED?" Sonya asked without attempting to hide the frustration in her voice.

"Oh, that. Yeah, well yesterday I went everywhere I could think of to find work, and nobody is hiring part-time help. I know we need the money, and I'm trying, but part-time work is hard to find right now. I was thinking that if I could get rid of this high school thing, then I could look for a real, full-time job. We need the money, Mom."

"But don't you want to get your diploma?" she asked somberly. "You have made it so far. You're almost there."

"Yeah, I guess, but I really just wanted the diploma for you. Not all jobs require one, and a GED can get me what I need. Mrs. Thomas says she thinks I won't have any problem getting into the program, and then it's up to me how long it'll take to get ready for the test. She thinks if I apply myself, I can get it done quickly."

"That's what she told me too. I hate the idea of you not graduating, though, Cole."

"Did Mrs. Thomas say anything about my grades?"

"She said they aren't great. Shouldn't interims have come out by now? I never saw it."

"I know. That's because they are a lot worse than not great. I'm failing everything, and some of it is so low I don't think it's possible to bring the average up in time."

"Sounds to me like you already made your decision. Can we at least take a week or so to think about it?"

"Sure, Ma. Where did you say you're working this weekend?"

"I'm at the DMD lake house this weekend."

"The wheelchair kids?"

"That's not very sensitive, Cole, but yes. I need to get there early tonight to go over the medicine schedule and special directions for each child. Shelby is splitting it with me, and she has been there all day getting things set up and she needs to bring me up to speed."

"Don't forget to hang your stethoscope around your neck," Cole teased.

"You joke, but I have one in my bag. Are you going to be okay this weekend, Cole?"

"Of course. I'm a big boy, Mom. Go ahead. I'm fine."

"Keep looking for a job, honey. Maybe you can find one, and it will all work out."

"I will. How's your head, Ma? I can drive you to the lake if you need me to."

"Thanks, but then you'd have to come get me in the morning. I'll be fine. It's easing up a little bit. Please behave yourself while I'm gone."

"I will. Go do your nurse thing. I'll see you tomorrow."

Sonya just nodded, grabbed her bag and said, "I left dinner in the fridge for you. Three minutes in the microwave should do it. Have a good evening, Cole."

Chapter 23

Eve had seen a lot of things in her life, but this was new. Carloads of people, wheelchairs, and even a couple of service dogs lined the circular driveway at the lake house. A flurry of activity surrounded each arrival. Volunteers from a local church, the parents of each special needs child, and two nurses helped the host family bring in suitcases and supplies for their boys. They unloaded BiPAP breathing machines and set them up next to beds labeled with each boy's name. They placed special wedge pillows on the beds of boys who needed to sit up while sleeping, and they assigned spots for the service dogs' needs. The nurses logged in medications and wrote their administration schedules on a large whiteboard in the playroom that served as the nurses' quarters for the weekend.

Eve found the amount of specialty items staggering. The parents and nurses were undaunted though, and before long everything was situated in a logical place for its eventual use. Of course, the boys didn't care one bit about any of that. They were too busy laughing while catching up with each other and telling stories. Danny, Jordan's sixteen-year-old roommate from New Jersey, was especially happy to be there. His cute round face and rosy cheeks lit up with a beautiful smile that was infectious to everyone around him.

Eve didn't want the evening to end. Compassion for the kids and their families overtook her. Except for the soft whine of an electric wheelchair passing by, one would have no indication that each boy dealt with a life-threatening disease.

Eve wandered into the living room and focused her attention on two fourteen-year-olds who had been assigned to room together for the weekend. The conversation between them appeared effortless. It was then that she truly understood when Jordan said earlier that day: "The best part about these guys is that they get it. They truly get it." In that one simple statement, Jordan summarized a lifetime of heartache, struggle, and anger mixed with love, laughter, and acceptance. Eve realized that these boys would be friends for life, no matter how long those lives happened to be.

As she watched Austin and Caden, Eve noted the similarities between them. They were both shorter than boys their age, and each had the same full preciously pinchable cheeks as Jordan's and Danny's. Austin, from south Louisiana, was dressed entirely in camouflage, including a camo baseball cap. In his southern accent he told his friend about the new robotic arm that he now used to eat by himself. He was even able to put his cap on and off now. Caden was listening intently and fantasizing about a robotic arm that would allow him to throw a football to teammates at school.

"You still the manager of the football team?" Austin asked.

"Of course. I will never give that up, and there isn't anyone that is brave enough to take it away from me," Caden laughed.

Eve knew she had one of the few faces unfamiliar to the boys and didn't want to be too intrusive, so she passed Austin and Caden and strolled into the living room. There she found Henry and Jordan laughing about some memorable play they both saw in a televised LSU football game. Eve expected that both boys were wearing purple and gold jerseys in expectation of seeing each other. Robert from Romania, Henry's roommate, sat quietly listening to his friends get hysterical over LSU, but he had nothing to offer to the conversation. He wasn't even sure what LSU stood for, except that it was an American college football team.

"Hi," Eve said as she put her hand on the boy's shoulder in greeting. "Your name is Robert?"

"Yes ma'am." The boy looked up from his chair and was immediately taken with Eve.

"I understand you are from Romania."

"Yes ma'am. Have you ever been there?"

"Da, am. Îmi place acolo," she responded.

Robert's bright blue eyes lit up and his smiling face beamed. "Really? You have been there and you loved it? Where have you been?"

Eve and Robert chatted for a while in Romanian, sharing their experiences and laughing at each other's stories. Adam appeared by his wife's side but didn't want to interrupt the bonding between Eve and this special young man. So he just waited and listened, understanding every Romanian word that passed between them. When Eve noticed him, she introduced Robert.

"Adam și Eva? E amuzant," Robert laughed.

"Yeah, we get that a lot," Adam admitted, switching the conversation to English.

"What have you been doing?" Eve asked her husband when they ran out of things to talk about.

"Oh, Mr. Elliott wanted help moving the deck furniture off the patio to be ready for the wheelchair soccer game tomorrow. Most of it is cast iron and glass, so it would be tricky to move by himself. He didn't want to ask his wife because she had so much else to do, and he said his son Sam just can't do it anymore."

"How do you guys play soccer?" Eve asked Robert.

"It's actually a thing. People that play power soccer seriously have a soccer guard that attaches to the chair. We don't have that. Instead, we just kind of run into the ball and try to make it bounce in the right direction. The patio is not as wide as a real court, but we don't have as many players, so it works out all right. One goalie guards the entire end of the patio, and we have two players on each side. Sam is the referee 'cuz he doesn't have a wheelchair. The adults stand along the sidelines to kick the ball back into play if it gets away from us. It's really fun," Robert explained.

Later, Eve helped Elise, Mrs. Elliott, and a couple volunteers from the church prepare the food. They put bowls of fresh fruit around the house for snacks throughout the weekend and cut up veggies they stored in small Ziploc bags in the refrigerator. Eve was delighted to see the low calorie, health-conscious selections, "I'm pleasantly surprised to think that teenagers today would be willing to eat like this."

Mrs. Elliott picked up on the comment and replied, "All the boys are in the same boat, calorie speaking. None of them are able to exercise or even move around much, and eating normal teenage food causes a lot of problems for them. Weight gain is an obvious issue, but we all want these boys to live every day they possibly can. Promising to provide them with healthy food is one reason that parents are willing to put forth the effort and money to get them here every year. Most of the moms send us low-cal recipes that their sons like, and we pick the best ones and try them."

"That's a great idea!" Eve exclaimed.

"Parents really get into it. Collecting recipes gives each family new ideas for the following year. We print all the recipe ideas and hand them out to everyone when they leave."

"You could publish the recipes, or post them online for other families," Eve suggested.

"We do some of that," Mrs. Elliott said. "I keep saying I want to combine all of the recipes from every year we have done this, but I never get around to it. I know the kids would rather eat pizzas and hamburgers all weekend. But on Sunday afternoon, just before they leave, we have a huge ice cream social with all the fixings, and we even have brownies as an extra treat. Tonight, it will be frozen yogurt for dessert, but they know they get the full-fat fun stuff soon, so they handle it pretty well."

"I actually like frozen yogurt better than ice cream," Eve commented and Mrs. Elliott agreed.

While the women were working on the food and the others were socializing, Adam found Jordan and Michael. They went out on the patio on the lakeside of the house together. "That's beautiful, isn't it?" Adam commented.

"It sure is," Michael admitted. "My favorite time out here is at sunset when the exquisite orange and pink colors reflect off the lake, and the water is as slick as glass. It's so peaceful and beautiful."

"Yeah, yeah," Jordan said. "Pretty water. Pretty sunset. Can I go back in now? I don't want to miss anything."

Adam responded before Michael could fuss at his son. "Sure, you can go in if you want to. I just asked you to come out because I feel like God is laying it on my heart to pray over this weekend. Since you and your dad are the only ones who know who I truly am, I wanted you to be with me when I pray. But it's your choice, Jordan."

The boy looked at the smugness on his father's face. "Uh, yeah. Sorry, Adam. I'll stay."

All three men closed their eyes and bowed their heads. Jordan snuck a peek to see if anyone was trying to hold his hand. When he noticed Adam's clasped together and hanging loosely in front of him, he relaxed in his chair and tried to concentrate on Adam's words.

"Father, we love you and are humbled to come before you tonight. We thank you for this time to be together and for Jordan to reconnect with friends who are so dear to him. We ask for your divine protection over this group of young men and their families this weekend and praise your name above all others. Amen."

The other two echoed the amen, but the quizzical look on Jordan's face made Adam smile. "What?"

"Uh, nothing," Adam kept his eyes locked on Jordan's, expecting more. "I mean, that's it? I kinda expected something a little more . . . I don't know . . . flowery!"

"God knows your heart, Jordan. You don't need to ramble on and on. Just tell him you love him and appreciate what he's done for you, and tell him what's on your mind. He already knows, but he likes to hear you say it."

"I guess. Hey, does that mean that God will get your angels to hang out with us all weekend? Or will they go with you when you leave?"

Adam laughed. "Well, first of all, let me clear up the fact that they aren't *our* angels. They serve God and God only. They have just been assigned to assist us within the parameters of God's will for us and for those around us."

"Right, right, but you know what I mean," Jordan interjected. "They're around here right now, aren't they?"

"Yes, I'm sure they are close. Oh, look at that," he said, pointing. "I love it when I get to see those!"

"Fireflies!" Jordan exclaimed. "Me too. I remember catching them when I was really little. I never could run, so I never could catch any by myself. I remember Dad would carry me and run to where I could reach one. I would watch it on my hand until it took off again. When I got too big for Dad to carry me around the yard, Amy would run around trying to catch them for me." Jordan paused and his father nodded. Then he continued. "She would put as many as she could catch in a jar with grass in the bottom and holes in the lid and bring them to me to hold and look at. Do you remember that too, Dad?"

Michael smiled, "Of course I remember that, son. It's one of my fondest memories of your childhood. It was one thing that allowed me to see the bond between you and your sister. She knew you loved fireflies and couldn't chase them on your own, and you knew that she caught them especially for you. It was one thing that the two of you did that always made me feel close as a family. No matter what one of us needed, another of us would step up and help out."

"I never thought about it like that," Jordan admitted. "I just thought I was looking at bugs in a jug," he laughed. "But from now on, I'm going to look at lightning bugs in a different way. I am going to remember what you said about how important family is every time I see one from now on, Dad." Jordan smiled up at his dad in a rare, vulnerable moment. Michael's eyes teared up when he bent down to pull his son close to him in a hug.

After dinner, the kids strategized about their Minecraft world. They wrote down some preliminary ideas, chose teams, then adjourned to the family room to watch a movie on the expansive 110-inch television. The adults cleaned up and helped the nurse get things ready for bedtime.

After getting everyone dressed, medicated, lifted out of their chairs, and situated in bed as comfortably as possible, Adam and Eve joined Elise and Michael in the kitchen. They were debating the duration of leaving the BiPAP machines off the kids. Everyone agreed that they should allow the kids to talk until they were sleepy enough to drift off. But nobody wanted them sleeping without the breathing assistance, so they debated as they did every year whether to go in and strap the face masks on the kids after an hour or after the talking ceased. As always, it was left up to the nurse's discretion.

After a while, the night shift parents showed up, releasing Elise and Michael until Sunday afternoon. All exchanged hugs and best wishes and made sure everyone had cell phone numbers at the ready. Adam and Eve were sad to leave but commented that it had been a wonderful and enlightening experience for them.

Chapter 24

Sonya decided not to take anything else for her migraine before she made the final sweep through all the rooms. She loved working at the Elliott home, and after she made peace with her jealousy over the breathtaking house and the expansive lakefront property several years ago, she made up her mind to enjoy being a part of the experience. Even under the best of circumstances, though, the job was not without stress, and the Cole-induced headache that followed her from home would just not ease up.

Her room, as she suspected it would be, was once again set up in the playroom in the center of the southwestern wing of the house. Three bedrooms radiated from the playroom. When the Elliot children were younger, the layout was perfect for them. The two boys and their sister each had their own bedroom and bathroom, although the boys' bathrooms were connected in the center. The girl had her own full bath to herself, and Sonya suspected that was a smart move on the parents' part. All three bedrooms had a door that accessed the communal playroom, and Sonya suspected all phases of growing up had occurred there. She could picture couch-cushion-and-blanket forts, LEGO villages, and Hot Wheels tracks that later gave way to video games and stereo equipment. For now, the playroom was set up as a nurse's station, giving both Sonya and Shelby direct access to each room and to the six DMD patients who required their expertise.

Sonya completed her duties in the first of the three rooms, and even with a pounding headache, she had no trouble at all. Both boys were exhausted from the excitement of the day. Robert was fast asleep, allowing Sonya to secure his equipment without his knowledge. Henry was groggy, but he was awake enough to lift his head to help her secure the BiPAP face mask in place. Sonya hated to disturb him, but understood why their parents had agreed to allow the boys to talk until they fell asleep. She suspected that to do otherwise would steal a rare opportunity for them to bond.

Both Austin and Caden in the second room were sleeping soundly. Sonya couldn't help but take several long moments to look at them. All the boys were precious. Their chubby little rosy cheeks were typical of Duchenne patients as was the stunted growth. What stood out the most to Sonya, though, was their apparent acceptance of their situation. It was no secret to any of them that their time on earth was limited, but they seemed so happy. She knew that the retreat weekend pulled the positive out of them, and while there had to be other times when they allowed anger and tears to take over as a result of the cards they had been dealt, this was not the scenario that Sonya witnessed every year. She saw the acceptance of their circumstances, their love for their friends and family, and unbridled joy at spending time together. She also saw wheelchairs, mechanical arms, and breathing machines. Somehow, she just couldn't make sense of the conflicting images.

When Sonya approached the third and last room, she was conflicted. It was time for these boys to sleep, but Jordan and Danny were in a deep conversation. She couldn't know that the conversation was prompted by Eve's angel, Andel. He had suggested the topic for the purpose of having Sonya overhear it. She also didn't know that it was Andel's idea that she pull up a chair close to the doorway to listen to the boys until the conversation died down. She justified this by telling herself that she was not eavesdropping, she was merely allowing them to finish their conversation.

She heard Jordan ask Danny, "What do you think our bodies will be like before we get the glorified ones?"

"I don't know, Danny replied. "I asked our preacher, and he doesn't know either. But they'll be better than this one, I know that."

"I want wings like angels have."

"Yeah. That would be cool, but I don't know if we get those or not. Hey, we need to find each other when we get there."

"You know it! You better not be taller than me." Jordan joked, but got no response; so, he tried a different angle. "We can hang out and play football, or go hiking or something."

"Whichever of us gets there first has to promise to find the other one later. Promise?"

"Promise."

It sounded to Sonya like Jordan was trying to push himself up in the bed before he continued. "Mom's on this kick lately. She keeps making me memorize scripture verses that she thinks will be comforting. She thinks I hate it, but sometimes when I get down about things, the stuff I have memorized pops back into my head, and it comforts me somehow. Anyway, the latest thing she had me memorize is in 2 Timothy 2:10: 'I am willing to endure anything if it will bring salvation and eternal glory in Christ Jesus to those God has chosen.'"

"I haven't heard that one before," Danny said. He sighed, "Do you get tired of people acting like they need to feel sorry for you? It bugs me. I like my life. Of course, it's all I've ever known."

"It's like I always say, Danny. This disease isn't terminal. Life is terminal. Anybody can die at any minute in a car accident or something. I don't want to live life thinking I'm a victim. I'm just a human like anyone else."

"Yeah, I guess everybody has something to deal with." He paused for a long moment before he continued, "I feel bad about thinking this, but sometimes I want to just go ahead and go. I want to experience life in a place where there is no pain or deformity or wheelchairs. But I also don't ever want to leave here."

"What do you mean by that?"

"You know what I mean."

"Yeah, I do." There was a long pause before Jordan continued. "I don't want my family to go through losing me either."

Danny started to choke up, "My parents and my brothers . . ." He couldn't even finish his sentence.

"I know, man. I know," Jordan said softly.

Sonya entered the room quietly and, prompted by Andel, she asked the boys a very simple yet infinitely complicated question. "Guys, I sincerely hope you don't mind me butting in here, but I don't understand why you think you will be alive after you die. I mean, how can you possibly have healthy bodies *after* you die?"

It wasn't complicated to the teenagers with limited time ahead of them, though. It was Jordan who spoke up first. He simply stated, "To be absent from the body is to be present with the Lord."

Danny pitched in a thought as well. "Surely you have heard about the two thieves that hung on the cross next to Jesus as he was dying, haven't you?"

"Yes. I've heard that story," Sonya said.

"It's not just a story, Ms. Sonya. It's true. It's been documented in places other than the Bible. Jesus was a man who died by crucifixion, and there are records of the two men he died with. Anyway, Jesus told the thief who chose to believe in him that he and Jesus would be in paradise as soon as their time on the cross was over."

"But how do you know that you aren't just in a box buried in the ground when it's all over? It doesn't make sense to me." Sonya's headache had intensified to the point where she started to feel nausea overtake her. She put her hands to her head and commented about the pain before she pushed through. Her heart ached to hear what these boys could tell her, even if it was inappropriate for her to ask. Home care nurses are taught to resist invasive questions to any patient, but especially children. Somehow, she just didn't care. "Is there any proof for what the Bible says happens after you die?"

It was Danny who spoke first. "Have you ever heard of the transfiguration?"

Sonya didn't know if she had, but the term wasn't coming to mind. She just stood there sorting through what she remembered from her childhood visits to a neighborhood church with her aunt.

Danny decided to help her. "It was when Jesus took Peter, James, and John up a mountain, and he kind of changed into an angel or something, and Moses and Elijah were there with him. They had died a long time before that, but there they were. They didn't have regular bodies, but they were alive and with Jesus. Just like we will be after we die. You can be too, if you decide to believe in Jesus."

Sonya shook her head. "I don't know, guys. It seems like first you have to believe the Bible is real."

"Lots and lots of people have tried to prove it's not real," Jordan said. "Nobody has ever been able to find a single word that can be proved to be wrong. And I've seen angels before, so I know it's true."

Sonya didn't know what to say to that. "Alright. Let's just say I'll think about it. Right now, it's time for you two to go to sleep." She reached for Danny's facemask and started to put the straps over his head.

"Can I make a bargain with you?" Jordan asked.

Sonya didn't respond, so he continued. "If I ask God to take away your headache and also ask him to keep you from ever getting another one like it, and he does it, would you promise to take the time to find out about Jesus for yourself?"

Sonya laughed. "That would truly be a miracle. Sure, I guess I could agree to that, but there's no way. I've had migraines for years, and the doctors can't even figure out how to get rid of them."

Jordan closed his eyes, "God I ask you to take away Ms. Sonya's headache and to never let her have another one as long as she lives. And while you're at it, could you bring someone to her who could explain things better than we can? Thank you, God. Good night and amen."

Sonya just stood there looking at Jordan as he prayed this simple prayer. She laughed to herself at the innocent but misguided and unrealistic child. *The kid seems to believe all this nonsense*, she thought.

As she put on Jordan's headgear and turned out the light, she noticed that her headache had started to subside. *Nothing but a coincidence*, she told herself.

Chapter 25

Jordan was having a great time. He had been tricked into thinking that the low-fat, nutrient-filled breakfast pastry was a secret treat that he had gotten away with eating, and Romanian Robert, his Minecraft partner, was excited about the strategic planning he had done online before the weekend. But what really made Jordan's morning was that he had been named as captain of one of the soccer teams, which meant he would make all the decisions for his side. There wasn't much he enjoyed more than being in charge.

Sam, the only boy who was ambulatory and therefore without a wheelchair, was the designated referee. Since he lived there and knew the space better than anyone else, he explained the house rules and the specific hazards around the backyard patio. The adults had previously moved all the furniture and when it was time to play, they lined up on the sideline away from the house to retrieve stray balls.

Austin, the camo kid, made the first score of the day against Jordan's team when he expertly propelled the ball across the end of the patio. The day nurse, Shelby, who had never seen the game played before, stood awestruck when she saw everyone clap and cheer for the goal. It was no surprise to see Austin's teammates cheer, but even Jordan's team and all the parents whooped and hollered their praises. Austin himself wasn't able to clap or hold his arms up in triumph, but the smile on his face said it all for him. Sam took the ball back to mid-patio and rolled it slightly toward Jordan for the opposing team's captain's first contact.

Throughout the entire match, the service dogs Penny and Elly sunned themselves on the patio's upper level. Aware of where their respective masters were, there was nothing to do during the game so they enjoyed their time off. When the game was over and the parents served snacks, the dogs returned to their boys and, as all dogs do, hoped to be included in the snack experience. Neither was disappointed.

The rest of the day progressed uneventfully. It began to rain, and the boys were glad they had scheduled the soccer game early in the day. From two to four in the afternoon, Jordan spent his designated rest time watching TV while Danny took a nap. Afterward, they all made great strides during their second Minecraft session then enjoyed another delicious meal together. After dinner, they played cards and watched a movie. At ten o'clock, they all went to bed after a full day at the lake house. Sonya showed up about the time the movie started but stayed away from Jordan and Danny, which Jordan noticed, figuring she felt awkward because of last night's discussion and the challenge they presented her.

Bedtime was uneventful. The full day of spirited activity combined with the sound of the relentless rain pounding the roof helped the household to settle down quickly. Both Jordan and Danny were asleep when Sonya entered to check on them. After she finished her chores, she retired to her room and picked up a book she brought with her. Three chapters later, a crash somewhere overhead startled her.

Quick as a flash, Sonya was on her feet, wide-eyed and alert. A cacophony of clashing sounds and flickering lights screamed for her attention. The zapping sounds intensified and the lights went out. Somewhere close by she heard someone screaming, but with the howling wind and crashing rain, she couldn't tell who it was or where the screams originated. She took her best guess and felt her way to the closest bedroom. On entering, water hit her face and wind whipped around her. She needed help. And a flashlight.

Turning around, Sonya groped her way toward the master suite, yelling for help. She thought she could hear Mrs. Elliot yelling something in return, but the noise of the storm made it difficult to ascertain what the woman was saying. It wasn't long before Mr. Elliott and two bobbing flashlight beams approached. He handed Sonya one and took charge. He spoke calmly but loudly enough to be heard by everyone. "Guys, I know this is scary. We'll get you to a safer place, but first we need to know you are okay. When you hear me yell your name, respond by yelling back as loudly as you can. Try to remain quiet until you hear your own name." Mr. Elliott progressed through his roll call and each boy responded appropriately, some voices muffled by masks that hadn't been removed. Henry didn't respond though, and neither did his roommate, Robert. Both wide-eyed adults darted into that room first, knowing that none of the boys would be able to get out of bed or do much else to help themselves.

Several steps into the room, a huge branch jutting off from a tree had come through the ceiling of the adjacent bathroom, blocking Mr. Elliott and Sonya. There was no getting around it, and it seemed to have taken over Henry's entire bed, pinning him under it. Robert, in a bed on the far side of the room, seemed to be safe and away from imminent danger. Henry needed immediate attention. They yelled his name again but heard no response. With all of her might, Sonya tried to move the branch out of her way, but it wouldn't budge, and she started to panic.

Mr. Elliott put his hand on her shoulder and shined his flashlight on his own face. "Shhh. It's okay. Let's just be calm and listen."

Mr. Elliott turned his attention back to Henry. "Hey, bud, you okay? You and Jordan have a bunch of LSU games to watch soon. You think you can do that?"

Sonya listened hard for a response. She and Mr. Elliott both smiled when they heard a faint voice. "Go Tigers!" After another moment, "I'm okay, but I can't get this face mask off. Something is on me."

"I'll take care of him," Mr. Elliott said calmly. "You go check on Robert."

Sonya climbed under the branch she had been fighting. "Robert? Robert? Do you hear me?"

Sonya went from panic to laughter as she strained to hear. Robert had not responded, but she heard the unmistakable sound of snoring. When she shined the light on him, she saw that his BiPAP facemask had been knocked off, and the sixteen-year-old from Romania was oblivious to everything. He was snoring peacefully, and the tree was nowhere near him. As there was no power to run the machine anyway, she removed his face mask and checked again to make sure he was in no danger.

"Mr. Elliott, Robert is fine. If you're okay with Henry, I'll go to the next room and check on Austin and Caden."

Sonya almost ran into Mrs. Elliott and Austin's hysterical mother plowing their way through the communal playroom on the way to her son.

"Is Austin okay?" she shrieked. "Is anyone hurt?"

Sonya yelled over the chaos. "I don't know much yet. Robert is asleep and unhurt. Henry has part of a tree pinning him down, but he isn't hurt, and Mr. Elliott is trying to free him. Let's go, come on."

Sonya started to hear cries from the other boys. Some screams were muffled by face masks, but others were unobstructed and panicked. While the two women new to the scene ran to Austin's and Caden's room, Sonya darted into the other room to check on Jordan and Danny.

The two boys were unharmed. As she stood next to Danny's bed freeing him of equipment and blankets, she heard the scariest word of her life.

"FIRE!" Mrs. Elliott yelled from the adjacent room. "There's fire and smoke everywhere. Help me!"

Sonya yelled as loudly as she could, "Breathe through your noses boys, not your mouths. Close your mouths. Breathe through your noses." She shoved one hand under Danny's back and the other one under his legs and hoisted the 120 -pound boy into her arms. As quickly as she could without risking injury, she rushed him to the couch in the living room, where she found Sam pacing back and forth. Danny's dog Elly trotted faithfully behind the lady carrying the boy she was devoted to protecting.

"What's happening? Please tell me," Sam pleaded.

"I don't have time now, Sam. Please take care of Danny here. I'll be back as soon as I can." Sonya rushed back into the darkened chaos, moving out of the way for Austin's mother with her son in her arms.

"Mrs. Elliott has Caden, but the fire is in the boys' bathroom and seems to be coming in both rooms. Do you know if he got Henry out?" She didn't wait for a response, and Sonya didn't take time to give one. She stood for a long moment trying to figure out which direction to go. Maybe Henry was free and Mr. Elliott had gone back in to get Robert. Maybe he hadn't, but she knew Jordan had nobody else.

Just then she felt a wet nose on her leg and looked down to see Jordan's dog, Penny, at her side. She grabbed a bottle of water from the dresser near where she was standing and yelled out, "Jordan, are you all right?"

"Yeah, but it's getting really smoky in here. Who is left to get besides me?" he asked.

"I think just Robert."

"Please go save him first. I don't know if he knows Jesus or not. I'll be fine. Live or die, I'll be fine. But I don't know about him. Please go."

Sonya stopped breathing for a moment when she heard the boy's words. She knew there was no time to waste, though, with fire so close to Robert's bed. She gave the bottle of water to Penny, who readily accepted it. "Call your dog. She has water. Pour it on a blanket and breathe through that until I can get to you," Sonya yelled. She heard Jordan call for Penny as she ran off to help Robert.

Mr. Elliott had finally freed Henry and reached Robert's bedside about the same time as Sonya. His wife appeared with a fire extinguisher, and he directed Austin's mother to go help Jordan. After a few short minutes that seemed like days, all six boys and two dogs were relocated to the living room, office, and family room. Besides some coughing, stinging eyes, and some wet, ripped pajamas, everybody was fine. The fire was out, and although the rain and wind continued to wreak havoc on the southwestern wing of the house, every occupant was grateful, happy, and relieved. And sitting in the dark.

"Has anyone called 911?" Mr. Elliott asked the group.

Everyone looked around and most shrugged in response. "Guess I better do that, huh?"

His wife responded, "We got it out, though, didn't we? I emptied the fire extinguisher on it, and I didn't see any more flames."

Her husband found the phone and dialed as he replied, "I know, hon, but it can get in the space under the roof and spread pretty easily. We need to get it checked out." After he finished with the emergency call, he handed the phone to his wife, "You better call the parents. This isn't something you want them to find out when they come tomorrow for the Minecraft presentation and ice cream social."

"I guess you're right. We also need to think about getting the boys some medical attention. Smoke inhalation is nothing to take lightly with anyone, but especially with these guys," Mrs. Elliott said thoughtfully.

Chapter 26

Sam was fascinated by the firefighter hacking through the ceiling, trying to locate any signs of fire and attempting to remove tree debris. He had been fussed at several times to stay out of the way, but ultimately his mother just brought him a chair and told him he could watch as long as he didn't move any closer. It was nowhere near close enough for Sam, but he knew he better comply or he wouldn't be able to see anything at all. So, he sat wide-eyed while everyone else tried to resume sleeping.

Adam and Eve arrived at close to three in the morning with Jordan's parents. The firefighters determined that everything was safe and the small fire was extinguished effectively. In the damaged wing of the house, the power was off, and Mr. Elliott made plans to call an electrician later in the morning.

Earlier Michael and Adam had gathered supplies to help keep out the elements. The firefighters wouldn't allow anyone near the roof, so they took the plastic from the men and tacked it into place for them. Michael and Adam went through the bedrooms and gathered everything they thought the boys would need. All the wheelchairs except Jordan's and Robert's had been relocated, and Sonya had done a great job saving all the medications and BiPAP machines. When they were satisfied that no life-preserving items were left behind, the men did what they could to seal off the damaged wing from the rest of the house.

Sam helped too since the firefighters had finished their work, and the show was over.

Before encouraging the kids to go back to sleep, Sonya made her rounds. She went to each boy and asked him to breathe deeply while she listened through her stethoscope. She detected no problems, but realized a doctor in a proper facility could give a better prognosis. She recommended to each set of parents that they call their doctors in the morning and take their boy to be checked. Everyone seemed to be all right, but with each of their varying levels of special circumstances and health challenges, she didn't want to make a blanket assessment.

Mr. Elliott was the one who had the most to say, and he spent the majority of time talking. First, he thanked everyone for the help that they offered and apologized for the inconvenience, although no one could argue it was his fault. He expressed guilt about not removing the tree he knew was too close to the house. Before this incident, he said he justified to himself that the tree was healthy and beautiful, and he simply didn't want to remove it. He told the group that he deeply regretted that decision and asked for their forgiveness.

When he was done apologizing and expressing his appreciation for the teamwork, he launched into his personal experience. "It was the weirdest thing. Henry was pinned under the tree branch. Fortunately, the trunk landed in the bathroom between the two bedrooms, away from everyone, but the branch that came through the wall into the first bedroom was huge. It angled downward, toward the floor, and flipping it off Henry was impossible. I kept trying to pull the smaller branches and break them off, but they just snapped back into place. When I was finally close enough to Henry, I could tell there was no way I'd be able to pick him up."

Jordan looked at Henry, who was smiling. It looked to Jordan as if Henry knew something the others didn't, like someone who knows the punch line but doesn't want to ruin it for the joke teller. Henry's expression made Jordan interested in hearing the rest of the story.

Mr. Elliott continued. "I decided to pull Henry horizontally off the bed and lower him closer to the floor. I thought the bed would keep the debris out of our way, and if I could maneuver ourselves under the branches and move backward until there were no obstacles, I might be able to get to a place where I could stand and find our way to the door. So I wedged my arms under his back and legs and pulled straight backward. That worked like a charm, and for a moment I enjoyed the brilliance of my problem-solving skills. I was in an awkward squatting position, but I thought I could crab-walk backward a few steps until we were in the clear, and then I could stand and look for the best way out. It was working until I somehow got stuck between the bed and Henry's immovable wheelchair. Even if someone came to help me, I don't know what they could have done. We were pinned, with me squatting between the tree branches and the wheelchair, and the wheelchair wedged against the wall. My legs had started to shake from strain, and Henry was getting heavier by the minute. I knew I needed God's help, so I called out to him, 'God please help me.' And he did! It was amazing."

Henry chimed in, "I swear I even felt his hands on me."

Mr. Elliott looked at the boy, "You did? I did too. My legs grew stronger, and I was able to push myself into a standing position with Henry in my arms, and the tree seemed to be supernaturally lifted out of my way. As soon as we got to the doorway, I heard it fall back into place. I promise, guys, I am not making this up. It was incredible."

Jordan was trying everything he knew of to catch Adam's eye, but he was too busy playing with the service dogs. When he looked at Eve, his expression said everything he wanted it to. She winked in response as if to say, "Yep. Angel to the rescue!" His expression changed to a smug *thought so*!

Sonya was sitting with her head in her hands and her elbows digging into her thighs when Eve approached her. "How are *you* doing, Sonya? The past few hours must have been difficult for you."

Sonya wiped her eyes and sat up straighter. She tried to smile. "No, I'm fine. Crazy night though, huh?"

"The way you were sitting a moment ago, it looked like maybe you had a headache. Can I get you something for it?"

Sonya smiled. "Actually, no. I guess that pose is from habit. I always have a headache, and sitting like that is the only thing that seems to relax me. But I don't have one now, and that's what's bothering me."

"You are bothered because you don't have a headache?" Eve repeated, thinking that she had heard it all before. Still, that was a new one.

"It's nothing. Is there anything I can do for you, Eve? I can make you a cup of coffee. I'm sure you could use some caffeine to make it through with no sleep to speak of," the ever-mindful nurse offered.

"No, I'm ok, but I *am* still interested in this headache thing. Why would it bother you that you don't have a headache?"

"It's just weird, is all. It's really nothing. You'll think I'm crazy."

"Maybe, but why don't you try me? Maybe I was sent to sit beside you tonight and talk to you about weird things. You never know."

Sonya was speechless. Her eyes started to tear up, and all she could only respond with an unintelligible noise.

"I'm sorry, Sonya. I didn't quite catch that."

"Uh, okay, I'll tell you," she sniffed. "Not because I believe the kids, but because I have to tell someone, and you seem to want to know." She took a deep breath and looked into Eve's eyes. "You are going to think this is crazy, but Friday night, when I put the boys to bed, I had a strange conversation with Jordan and Danny. They were talking about the bodies they are going to have *after* they die. I asked them why in the world they thought that. I mean, after you die, you're in a box, and you're soon gone. What does the Bible say about that? 'Dust to dust,' I think." She plowed on to get all of this out before she lost her nerve, "They are convinced that they'll be alive after they die, and they acted like they're looking forward to it."

Eve smiled and took advantage of the slight pause, interjecting a question when Sonya stopped to take a breath. "But what does this have to do with your headache?"

Sonya relaxed significantly. The headache was a safe topic; bodies after death was not. It was insane, and she had taken a huge risk verbalizing this craziness. Oddly enough, it didn't even seem to faze Eve. All she wanted to know about was the headache. "When I was listening to their body argument, they realized I don't believe it like they do. So Jordan made me agree to a challenge." She paused. Eve waited. "He said that if he could get God to take away my headaches, then I needed to agree to find out about Jesus." Eve smiled. "And he prayed and told God to never let me have another migraine." She paused again. "And he asked God to bring someone to me who could explain things better than he could."

"And not only do you not have a headache like you normally would on a night like this, I just said I was sent to sit beside you tonight and talk to you about weird things."

"Well, yeah. You see why I'm a bit perplexed."

"I do. I also know about what you are seeking to learn. I am willing to talk about anything that interests you, and I'll do my best to answer your questions. Or, if you'd rather, I can just listen. Whatever you need, I'm here. All night, with nothing else to do." Eve laughed, looking at the sleeping teens and parents strewn around the living room.

As the hours passed, Eve and Sonya discussed life after death. Eve explained that every person continues to exist in a different dimension when their life is over and they leave their fleshly bodies behind. The only decision is to choose whether to exist forever with Jesus or to live eternally without him. The problem, Eve said, was that not deciding leaves a person without a savior. Whichever way a person decides, the decision is final when the person dies.

Most of what Eve said resonated deeply with Sonya. But the pressures at home weighed heavily on her heart. Eve had offered to listen to whatever Sonya needed to discuss, so Sonya changed the subject to what she really wanted to talk about.

"My son is on my mind a lot this weekend, if you want to know the truth," Sonya admitted.

Eve seemed genuinely interested. "Tell me about him."

"He's a senior in high school but has never been interested in school. He doesn't want to go to college, which I am honestly relieved about. I don't have any idea how I would pay for it if he wanted to go."

Eve understood. "I realize that is a huge financial obligation to undertake."

"You got that right. I can barely make ends meet now, and there's no way he could afford one of those student loans. But thank goodness it's not an issue. He says he doesn't want to go anyway."

"What does he want to do?"

"Whatever gives him a paycheck, I guess," Sonya chuckled. "He had a job at a grocery store for a long time, but he just got fired. I don't know what is going on with him, but he's been getting into trouble at school too. I don't know what to do."

Eve thought for a moment. "You know, being a senior in high school with no clear idea about his future has got to be scary for him. Maybe he feels lost and confused." She paused for a moment while Sonya considered this. Then she asked, "What does your son enjoy doing? I mean, what drives his happiness?"

"Oh, that's easy. Music. But he's not going to make a living that way. It's too hard," Sonya snorted, waving her hand in the air as if the mere mention of making a living with music was ludicrous.

"Music? Is he a singer?"

"Oh, no. What I mean is that he's a drummer. He likes to write songs too, and he plays for a band that is basically a group of guys who live near us. They play in different places and small events, but they don't make much money at it. He's not bad, but what can he do with that?"

"I don't know. I would think there are more opportunities for drummers in Branson than in most towns in this country. Has he tried to audition for anyone before?" Eve realized this was probably the first time Sonya ever considered music as serious employment.

"No, I don't think so. He's mentioned a couple of ads he's come across over the years, but he's never tried to do anything with it. His time has been taken up with school, working his part-time job, or playing drums for one group of friends or another. He's always banging out a tune on something."

Eve thought for a moment. "Would you allow me to pray with you about his future?" She paused for a response and received a simple shoulder shrug.

Eve took one of Sonya's hands in her own, "Father, we love you and praise you for the protection you provided tonight and for the care you showed for these precious boys. Your daughter Sonya is coming to you this evening with a heavy heart in both her personal life and in that of her son's. We ask you, Father, to reveal yourself to her in your own way in the coming days and weeks so that she may come to know you intimately. Also, Lord, as with any good mother, she is concerned with her son's future, and we ask for your wisdom and guidance over decisions that need to be made soon as he chooses his direction in life after high school," Eve paused and lifted her eyes to meet Sonya's. "What is your son's name, Sonya?"

"Cole."

"Cole? Really?" She smiled, mostly to herself and continued. "We ask for your guidance over Cole and for you to show him a path that will lead him toward an interesting, exciting, and fruitful career that is also fulfilling. We are aware that you know his strengths and his shortcomings and that your path is the only one that gives true peace and fulfillment. We ask, Father, that you reveal this direction to this special young man. We love you and appreciate you. In your precious son's name, Amen."

Sonya repeated a weak, "Amen." When she saw that Eve was smiling at her, she asked, "Why were you surprised at Cole's name?"

"Because I have heard him play. He's quite talented."

"You heard him play? Where? When?" Sonya asked excitedly.

"We went to a church social with Jordan's family, and Cole was the drummer in the band that played there. I remember his drum solo and I commented that he is quite talented. I must admit, I don't know much about it, but I know it sounded great and the kids went crazy clapping for him."

"Really? I had no idea. I've heard him beat on things around the house, and I used to hear him practicing in the neighbor's garage, but I've never gone to a gig, as he calls it. He's really good?"

"I think so." Adam entered the room and saw Eve speaking with Sonya. "Hey hon," she asked him, "what did you think of the drummer we saw at Michael's church?"

"Oh, he was great! Very talented. Cole was his name, I think. Is that right?"

Sonya's face lit up. "That's my son!" she exclaimed.

"Really? Wow. Is he planning on doing anything with his talent?" he asked. "He looked like he was having fun up there."

"I know he'd love it, but from what he says, it isn't that easy to break into the business," Sonya said.

Adam looked at Eve. "What do you think about introducing him to Ike? If nothing else, he could maybe give some advice. I wouldn't be surprised if he offered some contacts in the area for Cole to meet or audition for, to be honest."

"Oh, my goodness," Sonya shrieked. "Really? You know someone with connections?"

"Not very well," Adam responded. "But Isaac is a friend of a really good friend of ours, and not long ago he treated us to tickets and backstage passes at a concert downtown. I also joined the band for a prayer meeting and got to meet the rest of the guys. They really are good men doing good work for God's kingdom. I'm completely certain he would treat Cole to the same concert experience he gave us if we were to ask him. He's a great guy."

Eve joined in. "He's a member of the Crying Rock Band. Have you ever heard of them?" she asked.

"Yes. No. I'm not sure. Can I call Cole and ask if he knows that band?" Sonya's mind was spinning in several different directions at once. She just hoped that Eve was a mother herself and understood.

"How about waiting on that for a bit? Let Adam get in touch with Isaac and see what he can do. That way, if nothing works out, Cole won't be disappointed. If it does, you can surprise him. Deal?"

Sonya was beside herself. "That would be so incredibly wonderful. Thank you so much." She hugged both Eve and Adam and rushed off to make something delicious for these wonderful people to drink, muttering something about seeing some hot chocolate mix and butterscotch shavings in the cabinet.

Chapter 27

Christopher entered the kitchen at Jordan's house and approached his friend's parents and Adam at the table.

"Chris, it's so nice of you to drop by," Elise said.

"I had to check on Jordan. The rumor going around was that a fire took out half of the lake house he visited. So, of course, I was worried about Penny."

"Heyyyyyy!" Jordan sang out entering the room and maneuvering his chair around the island. "I take offense to that." Penny entered with Jordan, but sat by Adam, placing her head on his lap, when she noticed him at the table.

"You're right. I was hoping your mom and dad were okay too." Chris teased. Jordan crossed his arms across his chest and stuck his bottom lip out. But his eyes were smiling. "Seriously, though, what happened?" Christopher asked.

Jordan and his parents took turns adding relevant details to the story until they were satisfied that Chris had the picture. "So, I guess the real question is, did you get the crown this year?" He turned to look at his friend in the wheelchair.

"No, man. That part sucked."

"Jordan! Watch your mouth," Elise exclaimed.

"Sorry, but it did, Mom. I totally deserved it for what I brought to the Minecraft world we built. It was awesome. But Sunday's plans kinda got sidetracked on account of the firemen and all. So, we didn't do the Minecraft world presentation this year."

"You still got the crown, though, Bud," Michael stated, looking a bit confused.

"Eh, not for Minecraft. We didn't do the presentation, so the adults never saw the cool stuff we built. And when they talked about the weekend at the ice cream social, they decided that Sam should get it. I guess they figured since his old room got burned up, it was the least we could do for him."

Adam interjected, "Sam also helped me and the firemen put up the plastic at about three in the morning, but you should tell him the rest of the story." Penny nudged Adam's hand when it appeared his mind had wandered from scratching her neck.

Christopher was confused. Michael said his son had gotten the crown even though Jordan said that a kid named Sam had won it. And Adam had hinted that there was more to the story, so Christopher just kept listening and trying to piece it all together. It was obvious that Jordan felt robbed and wanted to brag about his Minecraft contributions to make his case for earning the crown.

"I wouldn't be mad about Sam getting it for the Minecraft thing if we could have voted on the game like we usually do. But I went all out this year and feel cheated. All Sam did was dig a well. And he kept digging straight down looking for some mysterious new tool but all he did was found trouble. Seriously, man, it was bad. You never dig straight down!"

"Don't you think giving the crown to Sam was the right thing to do, since his house was damaged and his old room was destroyed?" Elise asked her son.

"I guess. But he got to sit in the fire truck too, didn't he? Why should he get both? I earned the Minecraft honor this year. That's all I'm saying."

Chris didn't want to upset Jordan any further or get him in trouble, so he decided to change the topic. "Is Amy around?"

Chris noticed Michael's attention shift in his direction and detected a subtle change in the man's eyes. When he thought about it, he realized that a moment ago he was just a friend of Jordan's visiting out of concern for his friend's well-being. With that one question, he had become a male visitor interested in a father's daughter. Michael appeared less comfortable with that scenario. "I think she's watching television with Eve," he said. "Why do you ask?"

"Oh, it's nothing, sir. I just tried to help her with an idea for one of her classes, and I was wondering how it was going. That's all." Christopher grew even more uncomfortable with the looks he received.

"Hey, sis! You have a gentleman caller!" Jordan bellowed and then burst into a fit of laughter.

When Amy entered the room and saw Christopher, her face lit up. "Oh, hey! I was going to call you. I really need your help." She grabbed his hand and pulled him into the next room while everyone just sat speechlessly and watched.

Eve sat on the couch with a bowl of popcorn. The television was off, and papers covered the coffee table.

Amy dropped Chris's hand and introduced him as she returned to her spot on the couch. "Eve, this is who I was talking about."

"Yes, we have crossed paths at the church and the park, but it is nice to be officially introduced. Hello, Christopher."

"It's nice to see you again," he responded.

"Right, I didn't think that out," Amy said, only slightly embarrassed. "Anyway, Chris, I need your help. I love the idea you gave me about teaching the kids to write dialogue using cartoon squares with thought bubbles. In the example you did for me, you drew us and illustrated what we were doing at the time. When you explained your vision for the kids, you said that the first thing they need to do is to create original characters. That's a lot harder for me than it is for you. I have thought and thought, and I just can't come up with anything that isn't ridiculously stupid."

"Don't be so critical of yourself, Amy," Eve interjected. "You have some good ideas."

"Trashcan Man, a superhero who teaches kids to tidy up after themselves? That isn't stupid?" Amy shrieked.

"Well, Christopher, I *do* suppose we could use your insight," Eve chuckled.

Christopher laughed. "Trashcan Man? Wow. Yeah, that's bad. Okay, let's see." He thought a moment. "You know, this *is* the most difficult part. But you want the kids to come up with their own characters."

"I realize that Chris, but I need to turn in an example of what I want them to do. So, I'm pretending like I'm the kid trying to make my own cartoon. I have no idea what to do."

Eve tried to help. "Christopher, when you did the one Amy thought was so good, you used real-life to inspire you?"

"Yes, ma'am, but it wasn't too deep. We were just sitting at a table, so I drew that."

"How about something on fire safety, and use Jordan's experience at the lake house?" Eve suggested.

"Did I hear my name?" Jordan asked as he drove into the room with a bottle of water and an apple. He wiggled the apple at Eve and took an exaggeratedly big bite out of it when he caught her eye. He couldn't stifle a hysterical laugh at his own wit and spit apple juice all over himself.

"You're such a dork," Amy said. Christopher nodded in agreement. Eve smiled at his attempt at an inside joke at her expense.

"What are you losers working on anyway?" Jordan asked.

"We're going to write a comic strip based on your weekend adventure at the lake," Amy answered.

"Cool. What do you have so far?" Jordan maneuvered his chair close to the coffee table to see what Chris had drawn.

"That's not bad," Jordan commented. "Except, I don't understand why the fire didn't do more damage." He looked at Eve and considered his words before he continued. "Eve, do you know that Adam prayed over the weekend before you guys left on Friday night?"

"I do."

"And don't you think it's possible . . ." Jordan paused to choose his words carefully, "that his prayer could have resulted in God watching over us?"

"Of course, it could." Eve said smiling.

"And if God decided to protect us from being burned alive, couldn't he have sent an angel to take care of the fire for us? I mean, if you listen to Mr. Elliott's story about the tree being lifted up off of him and Henry, it seems like one was definitely here." He smirked. "Or maybe he sent two angels."

"That's entirely possible," Eve said, still smiling at the boy.

Christopher stood up with the paper in his hand, waiting for a lull in the conversation to change the subject. "So, how's this, Jordan?" he asked when he got a chance and handed the strip to his friend.

The drawing had two panes next to each other, each showing one of the two bedrooms damaged by the fallen tree. The first panel showed the two boys in their beds, panicked looks on their faces, and tree branches protruding from the right side, with some fire near the ceiling. The second panel portrayed a reverse image of the same scenario but with more tree and less fire.

"That's about right," Jordan said, nodding his approval. "But seriously," he said, looking back at Eve, "the fire would have destroyed everything if something didn't stop it."

"How about putting one angel over both panels, protecting the boys?" Eve interjected. "I think that may be what Jordan would like to see."

"An angel, huh? Okay. Give it here," he directed. "I'll see what I can do."

When he was done, there was an angel over both cartoon panels with her wings stretched wide and her cheeks full of air. Wispy lines from the angel's mouth depicted an angelic puff putting out the fire.

Jordan scowled at the drawing. "Can you make it a man angel?" he asked.

Chris looked at him with a hint of annoyance.

"That's not a bad idea," Eve interjected. "Did you guys know that every time angels appear in the Bible, they appear as men?"

"Really?" Jordan asked.

"I've heard that," Amy stated. "And they're intimidating too. Every time one appears, somebody tells the person seeing them not to be afraid. Remember? Pastor Joe talked about it at the revival."

Jordan and Eve exchanged a look but said nothing.

Christopher sketched the edits until he was satisfied. "Well, he's not scary, but he's a he."

Everyone thought the drawing was great. They turned their attention to designing the layout for the next panel. Ultimately, they decided that Chris should draw an angel lifting a tree off a man holding a boy on his lap.

"Yeah, that looks close to how I pictured it," Jordan said when he was done. He handed the paper to Eve.

When it came time to fill in the thought and word bubbles, the four of them brainstormed about what the characters would be thinking or saying. After about ten minutes, Amy became visibly frustrated, grabbed the strip, and left the room with it.

Several minutes later she came back and handed each person a freshly printed copy. "Write whatever thought or dialogue you want in the bubbles," she directed. "When everyone's done, I'll put the ones I like together."

Jordan, of course, had the characters spouting sarcastic or comical dialogue that didn't really fit with the tragic circumstances. He knew that, but he was, as usual, going for the laugh. Amy's was a little too dark and depressing to make a good story. It wasn't until Jordan studied what she had written in hers that he realized she must have been worried about him. He felt his eyes watering and was surprised how much it meant that his sister cared.

It wasn't long before Amy was able to construct a usable strip. Everyone's ideas added a different viewpoint, so the dialogue would be varied and the artwork was impressive.

"All I have to do now," Amy said, "is to write a paper with the dialogue written out as prose. Thank you so much for your help, you guys. Especially you, Chris." She leaned over and gave him a one-armed hug and knee slap. Jordan rolled his eyes at his friend. *Good grief!*

"What about me?" Jordan whined. "I did more work than he did."

"What kind of work did *you* do?"

"I starred in the episode. See me right there? I was providing content!"

"Fine, dork. Thank you too." Amy wrinkled her nose up at him and he smiled.

"I do have a question, though, Chris." Amy said. "I thought the idea was to create a character that could be given prompts throughout the course."

"Hmmm," Christopher thought. "Well, that was my idea and I really do think you can make it work, but I guess you can use situations as well, like our lunch or the fire story here."

"I like the idea of the characters. I just need to come up with some. Do you have any suggestions?"

"Trashcan Man?" Chris chortled. "No matter what situation you put him in, he can worry about tidying it up!"

Amy grabbed a pillow from the couch and threw it at him.

Eve was holding the strip in her hand, with an odd look on her face. "You know Christopher, there might be a market for this. People who run Sunday school classes for young children are always looking for material. You could create a workbook with Christian comic strips based on well-known Bible stories, and at the bottom of the page have a place for kids to write about what happens in the stories."

Christopher appeared interested in her idea. "That would be a lot of fun to do, but I wouldn't have any idea how to market something like that."

"I know someone you could talk to if you're interested. Getting a strip published could be a portfolio builder if nothing else."

"I'd buy one," Jordan joked. "I certainly wouldn't do the work, but I'd buy it for the comics."

"But would you keep it in a protective sleeve like your Batman and Teen Titans comics?" Christopher asked. "If he would, I think you may have a money-making idea, Eve!"

"Nah. You're not *that* good," Jordan responded. "Hey, what are you doing that for?" he squealed at his father, who had just entered the room and placed the Minecraft crown on his head.

"It sounded like things were winding up in here, and I just wanted Christopher to hear the rest of the story about this crown before he leaves. He should hear it, even if you don't want to be the one to tell it."

"I didn't think you got the crown," Christopher barked at Jordan. "You said some other kid got it. What's up with that?"

Chapter 28

"Ma? . . . Ma? Where are you?" Cole hollered. He quieted to a whisper when he peeked into Sonya's room and saw her bundled up in bed with the lights off. "Ma? You okay? I thought I slept through breakfast again."

"Hey honey," Sonya replied. "No, I just don't feel too much like getting up is all."

"Your headache that bad today?" Cole asked.

I wish I had a headache, Sonya thought. *At least then, it would be a normal Saturday morning.* "No, I don't have a headache this morning. Kind of weird both of us being home at the same time, huh?" Sonya threw the blankets off and swung her legs around to sit on the side of her bed. "You hungry?" she asked, rubbing her face with her hands.

"Yeah. Sorta. It's almost ten," Cole replied. "I can make us something if you don't feel up to it, Ma."

Sonya considered the offer and was tempted more than she wanted to admit, but she dug deep within herself and reached for her slippers on the floor by the bed. "Nah. Last time it took me six months to clean up after you. I'm coming."

Sonya hoisted herself out of the bed, pulled on her robe, and hoped Cole couldn't tell she'd been upset. "What do you have going on today?" she asked as they made their way to the kitchen.

"Nothing, really," Cole replied. "I heard there was a sign up at Home Depot saying they were hiring, so I thought I'd put in an application. But that's all until tonight."

"Tonight?" Sonya asked.

"Yeah, Ma. Don't you remember? Tonight Adam is taking us to see the Crying Rock Band in town. You set it up with him."

"Oh, yeah. That *is* tonight, isn't it? I guess I have a lot on my mind," Sonya said as she slid a glass of orange juice across the narrow kitchen island to her son.

"You can still go, can't you? It would be super awkward with just me and that Adam guy. He seems nice and all, but I don't really know him."

"I think Eve's going too."

"Same difference, Ma. You know what I mean."

"Yeah, I'll be there. It might be fun. I haven't gone to a show like that in a long time."

Sonya plopped down at the table with a bowl of cereal. Cole was rambling on about something, but she didn't know what. Every now and then she uttered a noise so that he would think she was listening, but she just couldn't tune in. He finally got her attention when he slapped the table right by her cereal bowl.

"Ma. What's going on with you this morning? Are you okay?" Sonya thought it was sweet that he seemed concerned about her.

"I'm fine. I just have stuff on my mind. Nothing you need to be concerned with, Cole."

"Is it money? I really have been looking for work. I'll find something soon." He said, trying to comfort her.

"Actually, with the job I had at the lake last week, we're good this month. I do hope you get something soon, but right now everything is paid. Really, honey, I'm fine."

Cole went to the refrigerator to get more milk for his second bowl of cereal and laughed. "You sure you're okay, Ma?" From the top shelf of the fridge, he picked up a lanyard with her work ID badge and office keys.

"Wonder how those got there," Sonya said without much reaction.

Cole put the lanyard in the bowl beside the door where it belonged, carried the milk to the table, and pulled his seat closer to his mother. "This isn't like you," he said pointing at the cereal. "We've both had a Saturday off only once in the past six months. You usually do a big thing when that happens—waffles and sausage and eggs. Today I had to drag you out of bed to eat some stale cereal. I don't really care what we eat for breakfast, but I want you to tell me what is going on. Please."

"I don't really know, honey," Sonya said. Her eyes teared up, and she wiped them on her bathrobe sleeve. "Everything is fine at work, and when you find a job it'll all be back to normal. Really."

Cole just stared at his mother and waited.

"Okay, I'll tell you," Sonya said softly. "But you'll think I'm losing it."

Cole just sat there and waited for her to continue.

"I can't get something out of my head that this kid said last weekend."

"Was he rude to you, Ma?" Cole asked. The concern in his voice touched Sonya.

"No. Just the opposite." Sonya pushed her bowl away and cradled a coffee cup in her hands while she stared into it. "The first night I was there, I overheard these two boys talking about what life would be like after they died. I listened for a while until I couldn't take it anymore, and I went into the room and asked them to explain it all to me. They seemed to believe with all of their hearts that they will be in heaven with Jesus after they die. They both looked forward to getting new bodies that work better than the ones they have now."

"Why does that bother you?" Cole asked. "You've always known that some people believe what the Bible says about that. And you can't blame kids in wheelchairs for wanting to be free of that, can you?"

"Well, no. But I had a really bad headache that night, and one of the boys prayed for it to go away and for me never to get another one."

"So?"

"So, it went away, and it's been over a week and I haven't had another one. Not even the slightest hint of one. I haven't gone this long without a migraine in . . . well, forever."

"Well, that's really cool!"

"It is, but that's not all. He also prayed for someone to come teach me about Jesus, and the next night Eve came and sat down beside me and started talking about Jesus."

"Okay, but I still don't see why you think having prayers answered is something to worry about. It's really pretty cool."

"There's one more thing, though. And this is what I haven't been able to get out of my mind." Sonya took a sip of coffee and put the cup down. "This kid . . ." The lump in her throat started to burn. She looked at Cole, rose from the table, and took out the waffle maker.

"Mom. What are you doing? We don't need to make waffles. This kid really got to you, didn't he? What did he say?"

Sonya took a deep breath and decided to get it out. She wanted to talk about it anyway. So she backed up from the counter, put her hands on her hips, looked directly at her son, and started to explain.

"The night the tree fell on the house was chaotic. I was the only adult back there with the boys until the owner of the house showed up. We had checked on some of the boys, but by the time we get to this kid named Jordan's room, the people in the next room were yelling about the fire. I was standing closest to the other boy, so I picked him up and carried him to a safer part of the house."

Cole interrupted, "You had to carry them?"

"Well, yeah," Sonya replied. "These kids are not ambulatory. They each have electric wheelchairs to drive themselves around. But with the power out, it was too dark for them to see, and the tree crashing through the middle of that wing made it virtually impossible to maneuver the wheelchairs around like normal. The quickest way to get them to safety was to carry them."

"Wow. I had no idea. How many were there?"

"One kid, the one who lives in the house, was sleeping in a room that wasn't affected. But there were six other boys, two each in three bedrooms. We needed to move each of them. When things were the craziest, we couldn't see anything. The women in the next room were screaming about the fire, and everywhere was filling up with smoke. Depending on the progression of their individual case, a DMD kid may not have enough muscular strength to cough mucus out of their airways and smoke inhalation would cause the lungs to become irritated. Just breathing that stuff in could kill them, Cole. I was scared for them."

Sonya sat down at the table. "There was one moment when I needed to decide who to help. I knew everyone had been relocated except for two of them. That kid Jordan yelled to me and asked me who was left. I told him it was just him and one other boy, and that's when he blew my mind."

Sonya willed herself to go on without getting emotional. She took a deep breath and continued. "Cole, this helpless kid told me to go save the other boy. The smoke was filling his room, and he told me later that he could see the flames through the doorway. So he knew that if I chose to help the other boy, he might not get out alive. He knew it, Cole! He even said so. He said, 'Please go save him first. I don't know if he knows Jesus or not. I'll be fine. Live or die, I'll be fine. I don't know about him, though. Please go.' So, I went."

Sonya searched Cole's face for his reaction. He was looking at her expressionless. "Cole," she exclaimed. "This kid was willing to die a horrific death because he didn't want it to happen to his friend."

"You mean, if his friend wasn't going to go to heaven," Cole added.

Now it was time for Sonya's face to go blank. Cole must have understood, because he continued, "Ma, he was worried the other kid wasn't saved. If he wasn't saved, then he would go to hell if he died. Since your boy knew he was going to heaven, he didn't have anything to lose."

"Didn't have anything to lose?" Sonya shrieked. "As far as he knew, he was probably going to die! I'd say that's a lot to lose."

Cole played with the cereal left in his bowl while he considered this. "Didn't you say that the night before all this happened that he and his buddy talked about leaving this world and acted like they were looking forward to it?" Sonya nodded. "Then maybe he figured he was ready to go, if he had to."

She just stared through the table and shook her head. "His parents were so proud of him," Sonya eventually said.

"I guess so!" Cole chuckled. "That's awesome. The Bible says that the greatest thing anyone can do is to lay down his life for another person."

"That's exactly what his mom said that night when I told her what her son had said. I didn't leave when my shift was over in the morning because I knew Shelby, the other nurse who was coming in, would have too much to deal with on her own. Anyway, the next day at their ice cream social, Mr. Elliott gave everyone who wanted to the chance to speak, and because I stayed, I got to hear it. Most of the kids wanted to tell their side of what happened and a lot of it was exaggerated."

"Maybe not from their point of view," Cole postulated. "Can you imagine? Being stuck in bed, with no way to get out of harm's way, with people screaming 'fire' and smoke filling the room? That would be terrifying for anyone. How old are these kids?"

"Uh, let's see. The two boys in the room where the fire was are both fourteen. All the others are sixteen, except Sam, who lives at the house. He's seventeen."

"Man. The kids where the fire broke out were fourteen years old! No wonder there was a panic," Cole said, trying to envision the scene.

"Yeah, well anyway, the kids all got to tell their part of the story. When they were finished, the adults spoke. Mr. Elliott had already told his story the night before, so he didn't say much, but the others did. Mostly the parents who had arrived later in the day spent the time thanking me and the others who helped get their children to safety. There were a lot of tears and hugs all around. When Jordan's mother got the chance to speak, she told the story that I just told you. She told everyone there that Jordan asked me to go help Robert, knowing full well that diverting me to the other room may cost him his life. The entire group sat there in stunned silence, all looking at Jordan."

"I bet he was a happy kid right then, huh?" Cole surmised.

"That's the weird thing," Sonya said chuckling. "He didn't seem to be the least bit interested in anyone even knowing what he said. He wouldn't even make eye contact with anyone. When it got a little awkward and he didn't look up, one of the mothers chimed in. She said that when she got in there to carry Jordan to safety, he and his dog, Penny, were both under the covers. His service dog took a bottle of water I gave her to the boy and he dumped it on his blanket. They were both breathing through the wet blanket to keep from inhaling smoke. When the lady told the group about that, Jordan looked up. He said that part was fun. He said Penny jumped right up there on the bed and climbed in beside him, under the covers."

"Did the dog make it out too?" Cole asked.

"Yeah. She's fine," Sonya said smiling. "She's a sweet dog. Golden retriever, I think. Anyway, when they were telling this story, the kid who was crowned with their special award for the weekend took it off of his own head and put it on Jordan's because of his bravery and self-sacrifice. It got a little emotional after that."

"I still don't understand what kept you in the bed all morning. Why would any of this upset you? It sounds like you witnessed some powerful stuff that most people never get to experience."

"I guess that's it, Cole. I have witnessed stuff, but none of it really fits with what I have always believed. There was such a feeling in the group that God had protected everyone. Mr. Elliott even thinks that an angel lifted the tree off of him. I mean, really? An angel was there to help? That's crazy."

"Why is that crazy, Ma? I know you have never believed in the Bible, but that doesn't mean that God isn't real and that he can't help us when we need it."

"Do you believe it? Do you think there could have been an angel there lifting trees off people and a God who will give these kids new bodies after they die?"

"Well, yeah, I believe it," Cole said slowly. "I learned about God when I went to camp as a kid, and I accepted him as my Savior then. And I really know in my heart that it can be true, but . . ." Cole paused.

"But, what, Cole?" Sonya asked, thoroughly interested in her son's insights.

"But I haven't been living my life lately the way I should. I know God is real and wants the best for me. But I haven't thought seriously about him for a long time."

"I don't know, Cole," Sonya said. "I've always felt that if I can't see it, I can't believe it. I may never be able to change that."

"Yeah, but Ma, last weekend, it sounds like *you did* see it!"

Chapter 29

It was four o'clock Saturday afternoon, and Isaac looked up from his spot on his couch to see Sly, the drummer from the Crying Rock Band, tearing into the living room.

"Guys, come here!" Sly bellowed to be heard around the house. "We gotta talk about something." Before long the entire band was standing around their drummer, wondering what had him so upset.

"What's going on, Sly?" asked Lance, the band's lead vocalist.

"I just got a call from my sister," he started. "My dad has had a massive heart attack, and they're rushing him to the hospital right now. All I know right now is that he's still alive, and I really want to be there with him."

"Where is he?" Lance asked.

"He's in Orlando," Sly said. "He had a small heart attack last summer, but this one sounds like it was a lot worse. My sister was hysterical on the phone, and I could barely make out what she was saying."

"You need to go be with your family, man," said Charlie, the band's keyboard player. "Don't worry about us for a second. We've got back up drummers—not as good as you, but they'll do. You need to go, man."

"But . . ." Sly started to argue.

"But nothing," Lance interrupted looking up from his phone. "I don't know if you can make it or not, but the last flight to Orlando out of Springfield tonight is at 6:25. It connects in Chicago, gives you an hour layover there and gets to Orlando at 12:46 in the morning."

"It leaves at 6:25? I don't know if I can make it to Springfield by then," Sly said, starting to panic.

"You gotta try," Charlie urged. "It only takes an hour to get to the airport from here. You don't need to stress over packing, just grab your toothbrush, some underwear, and some shirts and throw them in a bag. And if you really need something else, you can get it in Orlando. There will be plenty of down time. Trust me. I just went through something like this with my mom."

"Are you guys sure?" he asked, scanning his friends' approving faces. "Okay, thanks. I'm sorry, guys. Lance, can you book that flight for me?"

Less than a minute later, the four remaining members of the band were standing in Isaac's living room trying to figure out what they needed to do first. Lance was still working on booking the flight for his friend, so James, the group's acoustic guitarist, offered to call the back-up drummers.

"It's not even four-thirty yet, guys. We've got plenty of time. We don't go on stage until seven, and we're just down one drummer. We'll get that covered, easy cheesy," Lance said to nobody in particular.

"Should we send flowers or something?" Isaac asked, but nobody responded.

James slapped his phone to his leg and grimaced. "Brian's got the flu," he reported. "His wife won't even give him the message."

"Eh," Lance snorted. "Well, call Phil."

"Phil's in Acapulco for their anniversary," Isaac pointed out.

"Then that only leaves Ron," Lance stated sadly.

"You need to forgive him, man," Charlie stated. "It's been almost six months since he stole from us. It's over. Done. He admitted it, and I'm sure eventually he'll pay us back. Let it go."

Lance looked into Charlie's eyes. "I have forgiven him. Seventy times seven times. I forgive him every time I think about him and start to get angry. I forgive him every time we are tight with the bills and I think how much better it would be if we still had that money. I have forgiven him, Charles, but I haven't forgotten. And I'm not sure I am ready to trust him again."

"But what other option do we have at this late notice?" James asked. "We go on stage in just over two hours."

"I have an idea," Isaac said, "but it's a crazy one."

"If your cleaning lady can play the drums," Lance commented dryly, "I'd rather hire her than to call Ron."

"It's not my cleaning lady, but it's not far off," Isaac laughed lightly. "Do you remember Adam? He came backstage after a show and talked about our responsibility to God when singing praise songs in front of an audience?" The guys indicated they remembered but stayed silent, waiting for the rest. "Well, he called this week and told me about someone looking for connections in the business. So, I invited the kid to the show tonight. By all reports, he is a great drummer with lots of talent. Adam says he is finishing up his senior in high school and dreams of playing in a band full-time. I left him backstage passes at will-call to come meet the band after the show tonight. But maybe, if he really is any good, we could get him to play."

"A high school kid?" Charlie exclaimed. "Wow! Maybe we should change our name to the Crying Baby Band."

Lance spoke up. "Weren't you eighteen when you started playing professionally? And I think Sly was even younger than that."

The four men were silent for a long moment until Isaac spoke up. "Should I make the call?"

"Might as well," Lance said. "I don't really see that we have a choice."

Chapter 30

Cole couldn't remember ever being as excited as he was when he hung up the phone. He called Christopher and Jordan and told them that he was going to be the official drummer in the Crying Rock Band, and the show was scheduled to start at seven o'clock. They all expressed their excitement for him and said they would try to get tickets. Cole wanted to ask Chris to tell Lucy, but he decided that he didn't want anything to spoil his mood, which she could do with a simple expression he didn't understand.

Cole arrived at the venue early to meet with the band. He entered through the front door and explained to the usher who he was.

"Yes, sir," the man said. "I have been expecting you. Follow me."

The usher led the elated boy through a restricted entrance, down a long hall, and through a labyrinth of unmarked passageways. When they pushed through the last door that said "band members only" Cole's insides churned. He was terrified that he would be starstruck when he met them and come off like an idiot.

He had done all he could to prepare for the meeting. He was familiar with the band through their music and had researched each of the members online after Adam told him that he would be getting passes to meet them after the show. Now that the time had come and the band's expectations of him had increased, he worried that knowing their names and what they looked like would only get him as far as the introductions. He was going to be under the microscope with a band of veteran professionals, and he hadn't had even a minute to practice.

Adam had called him while he was driving to the venue and had talked him out of a full-blown panic attack. The kind man prayed for Cole over the phone, asking his Father in heaven to be with the drummer during his performance and to help him relax and play his best.

When he finished praying, Adam asked about the music the band plays. It calmed Cole's nerves when he listed how many of the band's songs he regularly played with his church praise band. *I can do this*, he thought when he hung up the phone.

When Cole was introduced to the band, his mind was spinning too fast to remember later what he said. Before he knew it, though, the men were slapping him on the back and doing what they could to encourage him. Even though there was only an hour before they went on stage, all five gathered with their instruments to allow Cole time to warm up and shoo away the nerves.

Lance asked if he was familiar with any of their music and appeared visibly relieved when Cole told him the names of the songs that he had actually played in front of an audience. They decided to start with those selections and then try some new stuff if that went well. To Cole, the hour they had to practice dissipated into a few brief moments, but by the time Lance said they had to stop, he knew he was ready. *I really can do this*, he thought.

Christopher and Amy were able to get tickets at the last minute, but their seats were far from the stage and nowhere near the others in their group. Christopher didn't mind at all, but he suspected Amy was disappointed that she had to sit with him instead of with her family. When he mentioned that, she laughed. "Chris, stop being so hard on yourself. I like hanging out with you, and besides, Mom and Dad aren't even sitting together. Mom is in the handicapped section with Jordan, and Dad is with Cole's mom and his new friends. Relax. It's all good."

Michael was excited about the seating arrangement. Originally, the plan was for Adam and Eve to accompany Cole and Sonya, but with the last-minute drummer change, one of the four complimentary seats became available. He felt fortunate to have it and the backstage pass that came with it.

Eve whispered something in Adam's ear and he nodded. "Hey guys. Why don't we go join Elise and Jordan for a moment and pray for Cole before things get started?"

When they were ready, Adam led the group in prayer. "Father, we come to you with praise and worship and a request for grace. We know that it is not merely a coincidence that the band needed a drummer on the night you orchestrated for Cole to be here. We pray for Sylvester's father in Orlando and hope that all who are close to him will be comforted and safe. Since we don't know the circumstances behind what has happened to him in Florida, we merely ask that you be with the family and that your perfect will be done in the lives of all of the people who gather there for Sylvester's father. We know that the opportunity for Cole to fill in for Sly is from you, since all good things are, and we praise you for this opportunity. Please lay your hands on Cole's shoulders and give him the strength to overcome any discomfort he may feel performing in front of an audience of this size for the first time. We ask that he understand the music he is reading, understand the cues the other band members are giving, and understand the power behind the beauty he will hear in the lyrics of this talented Christian band. We love you and praise you tonight as always. In your son's precious name, Amen."

Eve joined in the amen and smiled, but the two beside her still appeared lost. It seemed to Adam that Sonya didn't know what to think about any of it. She just sat staring wide-eyed at everything around her. And Michael admittedly continued to struggle with the concept of faithful prayer. "God's going to do what God's going to do," he had said to Adam at one point. "If it's his will to do something, why do I have to ask him to do it? Isn't he going to do it anyway? And if it's not his will to do something, why should I bother asking? He's just going to say no."

Adam had tried to help Michael understand, but it was still difficult for him to process. "We will never see the results of answered prayer unless we pray," Adam told Michael the last time the topic came up. "Sometimes God is just waiting for us to ask for what he wants to give us anyway."

Cole sat in silence, taking it all in as he waited nervously. When they raised the curtain, he lifted his drumsticks in the air and waited for his cue. From the first moment his stick hit the drumhead, he felt at ease. He progressed through the first three songs without a hitch and felt as if he could walk on air when Lance smiled in satisfaction at the job he was doing.

When Lance took a break after the first few songs to introduce the members of the band, Cole's life purpose came into view. He had never experienced anything like the way he felt when his name was announced across the huge auditorium and the enamored audience responded with applause. *They would have clapped for anyone who was sitting here,* Cole thought, *but I don't care. This is it. This is truly what I want to do with my life.*

As the evening progressed, Cole found himself at ease with the drumming. He allowed himself to be pulled into the lyrics of the songs Lance was singing. In one particular selection that Cole had never heard before, with a thankfully easy percussive beat, his heart filled with warmth. The man in the song had accepted Christ as a child but had been living for himself until he decided to rededicate his life to Jesus. The chorus, "and he welcomed me back like a friend he once knew, and loved me deeply as only God can do," stuck with Cole all night long.

When he went to bed that night the chorus continued to rattle around his brain, and he decided that it may not be a coincidence. He smiled at the thought that God may have stuck it in there for a reason, and he knew he was being prompted to act. Cole actually got out of his bed and knelt beside it, like he had when he was a little boy, and prayed the most sincere prayer of his life.

"God," he said. "Please accept me back. Thank you for saving me so many years ago, and please forgive me for straying. I have been following myself for so long that I don't know how to do any different, but tonight I ask you to show me how. I want to know you better, and God, I want my mother to know you too. I know you know that she has been struggling with faith and your existence for her whole life. I ask you to pull her close to you as soon as she is ready. And please help me to get her ready." Cole laughed, thinking that probably wasn't how you are supposed to talk to the Creator of the universe. "Goodnight, God. Amen."

Cole climbed into bed and pulled up the covers, feeling better than he had in as long as he could remember.

Chapter 31

Monday morning, Adam was sitting in the kitchen drinking a cup of coffee after Elise left to take Jordan to school. Michael came in and set his briefcase on the table beside him and sat down. "What are you and Eve doing today?" he asked his house guest.

"That's why I was hoping to catch you before you left for work," Adam replied. He always hated this part. "I needed to tell you that Eve and I will be leaving first thing tomorrow morning."

"Why so soon?" Michael asked, stunned. "Is anything wrong?"

"It's kind that you even ask that," Adam said. "We've been in your house for over a week now and in your way since we met in Egypt quite a while ago. Aren't you tired of us yet?"

Michael just looked at him as if he had lost his mind. "I never want you to leave, and if Elise knew who you two really are, she wouldn't either. You do realize that she is going to blow her gasket when she finds out I kept a secret that big from her for so long."

"Then tell her before we go," Adam suggested.

"I can do that?"

Adam tilted his head and smiled warmly. He reached out and touched Michael's arm. "I told you," he said softly, "that you can tell anyone anything you like. It just makes it easier for us if the circle is small and closed."

"Can she meet the angels?"

Adam laughed. "I guess. Listen, Michael, we do have to leave tomorrow, though. We can talk to her tonight if you like, but God has sent me a destination dream, and I have to be obedient and follow his guidance."

"A destination dream?" Michael asked.

"Yes. When we're done with one job, he sends us to the next one. That's why we don't have a home to call our own. He takes care of our itinerary and our destinations as long as we are obedient to his guidance."

"So, you were sent to meet me?" Michael reasoned.

"Of course. All we were told was to go SCUBA diving in the Red Sea with Gulf Divers on the day we met. Then, he brought you to us at the slingshot ride. Remember, you said you just kept feeling like you needed to go there, but you didn't know why? God was directing you then, and he is directing us now."

Michael raised both eyebrows, "Wow!" he said. "That's pretty cool."

"Are you ready to give your life to him yet, Michael?" Adam asked bluntly. "It seems you've seen your share of miracles and proof that he exists. Has it been enough for you?"

"I know it should be. I'm closer to that than I ever have been, but I'm just not there yet. I'm sorry, Adam."

"Don't put it off forever, Michael. You never know what is around the corner for you, but it's not something I can talk you into if you're not ready. God will wait. All I ask is that you listen when he's talking to you."

"I'd like to have a send-off for you tonight if that's okay," Michael suggested, changing the subject. "We can invite the people over that you've influenced while you've been here and have pizza or something."

"We'd like that," Adam replied. "We'd like that a lot."

That night, the Hammons' house was filled with people. Michael arrived in the midst of guests, carrying a stack of pizzas, sodas, breadsticks, and cartons of ice cream. Sonya had laid out a spread on the island between the kitchen and the dining room. Next to the paper plates and napkins were chips, a bowl of fruit, brownies, and different choices of soda.

"Put the pizzas here," she instructed Michael when she saw him balancing his load.

Adam prayed over the food when everyone had arrived, and the kids attacked it like it would self-destruct if they didn't claim their portions immediately. The adults flipped the pizza lids shut after they went through to keep it semi-warm for the second round. Penny followed Adam everywhere that he went.

While everyone ate, people straggled over to Adam and Eve to express their sadness over saying goodbye to their new friends. Cole had eaten a couple of slices when he noticed that Eve wasn't talking with anyone. He took a quick drink of soda to wash down the last bite and rushed over there before somebody beat him to her. While he was expressing his appreciation for Adam setting him up with the band, Eve stood up and gently jerked her head toward the sliding glass doors. Cole followed her outside.

"What's going on, Cole?" she asked. "I get the feeling there's something you'd like to tell us. I thought this would be more private."

Cole smiled, "Yeah, there is. After the concert the other night, I couldn't get the thought out of my mind that I have drifted away from God." Cole stopped himself, feeling embarrassed to be admitting something so personal to someone he barely knew. But something about the way she looked at him encouraged him to continue. "I accepted him as my Savior when I was a kid, but to be honest, I haven't thought about him much until recently."

"That happens. People get so caught up in their lives, they forget to look beyond themselves."

"Yeah, exactly. Well, after the concert, when I got home, I rededicated my life to him, and I just wanted you and Adam to know that you two are the reasons why."

"Eh, God nudged you and you responded. It wasn't us."

"Well, I wanted to thank you anyway. Could you tell Adam for me?"

"Absolutely." She pulled Cole into a giant bear hug. "I am so happy for you."

When Cole didn't act like he wanted to head back inside, Eve asked what else was going on with him. "It's my mom," Cole explained. "She's never believed in God and thinks that people who do are just stupid. She has always put her trust in what she can see and has never given it a chance." He paused to see Eve's reaction. She seemed to genuinely care, so he continued. "But Eve, that weekend at the lake with the wheelchair kids freaked her out. She saw and heard things that she can't explain, and I think she needs to talk to someone. She told me that you talked to her one time before. Would you mind trying again before you leave? I would really appreciate it."

Cole took a deep breath and waited. Being that vulnerable to a beautiful older woman he barely knew was difficult for him. Once he decided to talk to her, though, it seemed to fall out of his mouth on its own, and now he was relieved that it was said.

"Yes," Eve responded. "I can honestly say that there is nothing in this world that I would rather do. Where is she?"

Chapter 32

A little over twenty months later, Michael was devastated. He needed to get out of there, if only for a few minutes. He pushed through the double doors to the ICU and headed for the elevator. Elise stood in front of him when the doors opened.

"I got you some coffee, hon. It's decaf," she said, handing him a paper cup in a cardboard sleeve. He took it but didn't respond. "How are you doing, Michael?"

"I'm confused, if you want to know the truth. All this time, I thought I would be the strong one to pick you up and put the pieces back together when we lost him. But you seem fine. You're smiling and concerned about me, and you brought me coffee! I just don't understand. You are the one picking up the pieces of *my* life and putting them back together."

"Oh, sweetheart, you're doing great. Amy and I know you're there for us and will help us get back to some sort of normalcy."

"That's not what I mean," Michael said softly. "I mean you don't seem destroyed by all this. You almost seem relieved that he's gone. I can't handle it as well as you are."

Elise took her husband's arm and led him to a bank of chairs in the hall by the elevators. She sat first and he followed. "I'm not happy he's gone, Michael. I miss him like crazy, and our lives are never going to be the same. But at the same time, you're right. I *am* relieved."

Michael looked up from his coffee cup and into her eyes at her last several words. She continued. "I know you have trouble accepting the fact that God is real, but please, in the next few days watch for him. He will show himself to you, but if you aren't paying attention, you may miss it. I don't want that for you. I want more than anything for you to feel the love that God has for you and for Jordan."

Michael stared again at the cup of coffee cradled in his hands. "He is with Jordan right now. They're probably running and jumping and having a great time. I don't know, but I do know that Jordan is better off than he's been in a long time. The last several months have been so difficult for him that I am honestly glad he's getting a break from it now. Be happy for him, honey."

Michael was doing okay following his wife's reasoning until the last couple of sentences came out of her mouth. His anger flared, and he threw the cup of coffee against the wall. "I gotta get out of here for a little while." He slammed his hand against the elevator call button. When it opened, he got in and left Elise to clean up his mess. He knew intuitively that the coffee would be easier to deal with than the repercussions of his outburst, but he didn't have enough emotional energy at that moment to care. He just pushed the button to take him to the lobby and power walked his way to the parking lot.

The sun was shining bright, and there wasn't a cloud in the sky. Outside the hospital, the world was just a little too peaceful. It was obvious to Michael's broken heart that nobody seemed to be aware that the best son who ever lived had died a few short months before his twentieth birthday. Cars passed by on their way to some meaningless destination, and parents walked through parking lots arguing with children about things that didn't matter. It was too much for Michael to handle.

He sat in the driver seat without bothering to start the car or buckle the seat belt. He had nowhere to go, but he needed to be alone. He watched the hospital entrance for a while, not seeing the pain that others were in. All he could see was that everyone seemed unfazed by Jordan's death. How unfair.

Inconsolably sad, every emotion in Michael's body turned to anger when he saw a father, he assumed, walking beside his teenage son, who was driving an electric wheelchair through the entrance. He knew it was wrong to feel that the boy shouldn't be there if his son couldn't, but the jealousy and pain overtook him, and all the anger and sadness he had been holding back burst forth. He had no idea how long he sat sobbing by himself in his car.

When he was able, he went inside to the restroom, washed his face, and ran his fingers through his hair. He got into the elevator and punched the number for the ICU. He didn't even know if Elise and Amy were still there, but he didn't know where else to look.

When the elevator doors opened, Elise and Amy were in chairs in the hall waiting for him. They both smiled and greeted him with hugs. There was no sign of coffee on the floor or the wall, and Elise had even gotten him another cup. He wanted to think she was thoughtful for doing that, but to be honest, it made him angry. *How could she act like nothing is wrong?*

"My parents are going to hang around here a little while," Elise said. "My mom ran into a woman she wants to talk to. I think they knew each other in high school. Can you imagine that? Reconnecting here after all these years." The elevator opened and the three of them got in to head home. "I think I've called everyone I need to at this point," Elise continued. "Your parents left while you were gone. They said they would call people on their side of the family once they got home."

Michael didn't respond but nodded at the appropriate times. Amy looped her arm through his and put her head on his shoulder while the elevator carried them to the lobby. She held onto him until they got to the car. Michael thought that her strength was the only way that he made it there.

Chapter 33

Amy wasn't back yet from the airport run to pick up Adam and Eve for Jordan's funeral. Michael was nowhere in sight. Elise was finishing up in front of the mirror when there was a knock on the door. She yelled for Jordan to answer it and then caught herself. She started crying and had to start over with the eye makeup. The doorbell rang since the knock hadn't produced any results, and Elise was relieved to hear Michael respond to it.

When she came out of the bathroom, physically ready to leave for the church, she asked Michael who was at the door.

"Florist," he said. "Another peace lily. What are we going to do with them all?"

"I don't know. You heard anything from Amy yet?"

"Yeah. Their plane was a little late getting in, but they're almost here. I can't believe they are coming."

"Me neither. How crazy is that? Two biblical heroes and their angels are coming to mourn the loss of *our* son."

"I know. It took me a while to wrap my mind around who they really are too. I wonder how many 'greats' come before the title grandma and grandpa," Michael laughed and then stopped himself.

"You know, you don't have to feel guilty about laughing. Laughter was the thing Jordan wanted most from the people around him."

"I know. But it doesn't feel right today."

Elise came closer to her husband and gave him a hug and a kiss on the cheek. "You were—are—a great father, Michael. I know it's tough, but you'll get through it."

About that time, there was a commotion in the foyer. Amy had opened the door, and the two visitors entered with her, each carrying the same bag they had couple years prior." *I'd really like to get a look at what's in those bags,* Elise thought. *They've got this traveling-light thing mastered.*

There were hugs all around and a few tears before the uber-extended family left for the church. When they arrived, they were overwhelmed by the support of the community. No seats were left in the sanctuary, and people stood in every spare bit of space. Elise and Michael had reserved seats up front, but the printed brochures that the funeral home supplied had run out, so they didn't even get to see one until after the service was over.

The preacher who had known Jordan for his entire life choked up during his eulogy, which led to emotional repercussions around the room. He told stories about the boy he had grown to love and explained to the audience that it was time for Jordan's earthly loved ones to hand him over to God's care until they were all reunited again in glory. Everyone said it was a beautiful service. Elise pointed out that the song that played as the preacher greeted mourners was by the Crying Rock Band. She explained that Jordan had requested the song because it was the first one that his friend Cole performed with the band.

After the graveside service, Michael took a private moment to say good-bye to his son. He thought his heart was being ripped out of his chest as he stood by the casket that was resting on the straps that would be used to lower his only son into the ground forever. He leaned over and kissed the casket and dissolved into tears.

Adam came up beside him and put his hand on Michael's back. "He's not in there, friend. He might be here among us for a time, but he's not there in that box. That I promise you."

Michael stood up straight and tried to reel in the tears. He wiped his face with a tissue that Elise had stuck in his pocket and half-grunted, "I know, Adam. I know."

Back at the house, relatives from both sides of the family gathered around the food that church members had provided. Sonya was sitting by herself by the unlit fireplace until she saw an opportunity to speak with Eve. She stood, straightened her skirt and timidly walked toward the woman.

"Sonya, hello!" Eve said, pulling the nurse into a hug. "It's so good to see you. I heard Cole's song at the funeral. That was such a nice touch from a special friend. Is he here? I haven't seen him."

"No, he's not here, but he wishes he could be. He's on the road with the band."

"The band? Really? They kept him on?" Eve asked, delighted at the news.

"Yeah. He's been a roadie since you were here last, helping the guys move equipment around, selling T-shirts at concerts, and serving as a back-up drummer when he was needed."

"That's wonderful," Eve said. "I had no idea he was still working with them."

"About two months ago, Sly decided to leave the band to be with his mother in Florida, and they asked Cole to take his place."

"My goodness," Eve squealed. "He must be so excited."

"Yeah. He loves it," she said, smiling.

"Well, that's such great news, Sonya," Eve said. "But how are *you* doing? The last time we spoke, you were struggling with a lot of issues. Have you found the answers you were looking for?"

"I believe I have. That's really why I came here to the house today. I saw you at the funeral and was hoping I would get a chance to talk to you."

"Of course, sweetheart," Eve said, touching Sonya's arm lightly. "What can I do for you?"

Sonya swallowed hard and took a deep breath. "I was hoping that you would be willing to pray with me. I know now that God is real. I have seen him work in Cole's life, Eve. It has been amazing. Just before you came to town, he was fired from his job for stealing beer and getting so drunk he didn't know which end was up. After you left, he turned into a completely different person. He is always trying to get me to go to church and sends me inspirational things to read. I haven't told him that I've already decided to believe in God because I like the attention he's pouring out all over me."

Eve laughed. "I understand, but think how thrilled he'll be if you tell him the truth."

"I was kinda hoping you would do that for me too." Sonya smiled shyly. "Would you mind?"

"Sonya, it's what I live for. Let's go find some place a little more private."

Eve and Sonya prayed, and Caleb and Andel joined the angels in heaven singing praises to God in joyful acceptance of Sonya's declaration. Eve and Sonya contacted Cole through FaceTime with the news, and he was as excited as Sonya had ever seen him. He brought Eve up to date on his life and asked both women to pass on his condolences to the family.

When Eve returned to the gathering of Jordan's loved ones, she couldn't find Adam or Michael. She did see Amy, though, so she went over to see how Jordan's sister was doing.

"Have you heard from Christopher?" Eve asked after they exchanged pleasantries, and Amy asked if they could talk about anything other than her brother.

"Yeah. He couldn't make it because he's in college in Florida. It was too expensive to get a last-minute ticket, so his dad wouldn't let him come home. He said to tell you hi, though, if you were able to come."

"That's nice that he even remembered me," Eve said.

"Are you kidding? You made a big impact on him. Did you know that he rededicated his life to Christ after you prayed over his artwork the night that we worked on that comic strip? You said that he might be able to make some money with Christian cartoons and gave him a contact to call. Do you remember that?"

"Of course," Eve replied. "Did he follow up with it?"

"Yeah, and I think he has signed a contract to create some more work for the publisher. I don't know the details, but he spent a lot of time tweaking his ideas to fit what the publisher wanted. I'll give you his number if you want to call him sometime. I'm sure he can fill you in on it better than I can."

Eve was elated that Christopher decided to use his art to influence the next generation of children, and she was ecstatic that the young man had rededicated his life to Christ. Right then and there, Eve prayed for the talented college student learning about the cartooning business at Ringling College of Art and Design.

When Amy spun off to talk to a friend who dropped by, Eve again searched in vain for her husband.

Michael couldn't handle the small talk and the dreaded head tilt of well-meaning guests, so he went outside. Adam, also happy to leave the throngs of people inside the crowded, noisy house, followed, and they decided to take a walk.

The two men left the house near the end of the cul-de-sac on Michael's branch of the neighborhood. They walked down the street and crossed over the corner of a yard, and headed for a duck pond and a bike path that they hoped was deserted for the evening. It would be a nice place to walk and take in the fresh air.

They still had some distance to cover when they reached a field where the neighborhood kids played football. The sun was starting to set. The open field offered a great view to watch the pink and orange hues merge with the horizon. When the show was over, they resumed their trip to the duck pond, but after several steps Adam realized he was walking alone.

He turned to see Michael staring at the field. Fireflies started to gather in the center of the football field and the more that came, the larger the display.

Adam smiled at what he knew was going on inside his friend. "Looks like Jordan is finally getting to show off his skills on a football field," he mused.

"Do you remember what he said that night about fireflies?" Michael sobbed. Adam didn't respond. "He said he was going to remember how important family is every time he saw one. Do you think it's possible he's trying to communicate with me?"

"Absolutely," Adam stated, smiling.

Michael fell to his knees and exclaimed, "Okay, you win! I believe. Jordan, I believe. I love you, and I miss you, and I believe what you have been trying to tell me all along." He turned to look at Adam. "Will you pray with me? I don't know what to say."

After Michael accepted God's invitation for salvation, Caleb appeared to the men. "Angels in heaven are singing right now because of your decision. Be at peace, my son. Jordan is with us and he is mighty!"

Back at the house, when all the guests were gone, Michael found Elise and told her about the decision he had made. He told her what Caleb had said, and they cried together, holding each other so tightly that neither wanted to ever let go.

The character of Jordan is based on a student whom Beth Woods met in her upper-level geometry class during the 2017–2018 school year. The following was written by his mother, Lori Watkins.

As of this writing, Joseph "Seph" Ware is a vibrant seventeen-year-old living with Duchenne muscular dystrophy. While DMD slows him down physically, it does not slow his wit and personality. He loves to play the piano and the ukulele and to share his amazing vocal skills. Seph was selected to perform in the National Middle School Boys Honor Choir. He continues to take voice lessons. He is also an avid Xbox player and has many online friends. Seph participates in his high school Academic Challenge Team, Robotics Team, and he plays the keyboard for the marching band. Seph will make the rank of Eagle Scout in early 2020. He is active in his church, and he holds no fear of his future.

Seph has been blessed with many friends, some of whom appear as characters in this book. Some have DMD, while others have grown up with him and live with more typical challenges. The passage in the book about Jordan's visit to Microsoft is based on Seph's Make-A-Wish experience. Jordan's devotion to LSU and Batman is also based on Seph's life.

Seph plans to attend a local college when he graduates from high school in 2021. He wants to be either an architect or an engineer. Seph's prayer is that you "know who holds your future" so that you too can be excited about whatever the future holds for you. Please visit www.parentprojectmd.org to learn more about DMD or to help us find a cure.

Meet the Author

You can learn all about Beth Woods on her website, https://bethwalkerwoods.com, or follow her on Instagram and Facebook by searching for Author Beth Woods.